To Joe
Hope you
Jo Cook

MURDER, MAGNOLIAS, AND MANSIONS

MURDER, MAGNOLIAS, AND MANSIONS

Jo Cook

Library of Congress Control Number:		2008900063
ISBN:	Hardcover	978-1-4363-1549-4
	Softcover	978-1-4363-1548-7

This book was printed in the United States of America.

To order additional copies of this book, contact:
Xlibris Corporation
1-888-795-4274
www.Xlibris.com
Orders@Xlibris.com
45806

~1~

By six o'clock that evening, she had packed everything she could in her car. There were things she hated to leave, but the most important things were jam-packed in every available space, including the front passenger seat. *She certainly didn't intend to pick up any hitch-hikers.* It was going to be a sleepless night, so she finally stretched out on the couch with the lights out, her phone recorder on, and thought through her plan, making sure she had not overlooked anything. She lay there for a long time in the dark without feeling the least bit sleepy.

The phone rang, startling her. Looking at the clock, she realized she had dozed off. "Ten o'clock!" she said in disbelief, as she heard *his voice,* "Susan, call me when you get in. We need to talk." Panicking, she sat up in a fight or flight mode, then forced herself to calm down by taking deep breaths and exhaling slowly. *Slow down, you're breathing too fast* sang inside her head. Then, as if carrying on a dialogue with someone else, she said out loud, "Go, Susan, go!" She knew his habits, the way he thought, and how he would react to her departure—when he found out. She grabbed her purse, and without turning on the lights, went out, locking the door behind her. She started her car and eased it out into the street without turning on the headlights. When she'd gone a block, she turned on the headlights and headed for the main highway, taking the expressway north.

Listening to a novel she had on the CD player, the plot was enough to keep her alert for several hours. She'd been so engrossed in the story she hadn't paid attention to her gas gauge. Blinking at the headlights of approaching cars was a warning to her that she was tired, so she decided to stop at McDonalds and have a cup of coffee. Glancing down, she realized the gas gauge was on empty. *Thank God gas stations stayed open all night on the interstate!*

After filling up her gas tank and paying cash, she picked up a large coffee at McDonalds and drove one-handed back onto the highway. In Jacksonville, she found a used car lot that opened at eight o'clock, over an hour wait, so decided to move on north and try a small town lot. By eight o'clock she was miles down the road near a town called Waycross where she exited the main highway and found a used car lot. The salesman was not expecting customers that early. His feet were on the desk; he had a cup of coffee in one hand and the newspaper in the other. Startled, he looked up as she approached, then asked, "Yes ma'am. What can I do for you?" Susan answered. "I have a Lincoln I want to trade for a Maxima on your lot. Would you look at it and tell me how much cash I can get?" The man's feet were on the floor instantly as he asked, "The title in your name?" Susan replied, "Of course, I have everything you need." Thirty horse-trading minutes later, Susan drove the Maxima off the lot. The man was pleased, and although he didn't realize it, she was pleased. Her father had descended from a long line of astute horse-traders and her genes had carried on the tradition. The Maxima had fifty thousand miles on it, but the former owner had taken good care of it, and she now had twenty thousand dollars in cash to put into her business. Driving back onto the highway, she wondered if her destination would still be as quaint and as well scrubbed looking as it had been fifteen years ago when she and her father had stopped there for lunch. *Am I trying to recapture something from my past?* She thought about this and finally decided that what she wanted was a simple, uncomplicated life in a small town where everyone knew everyone else and respected one another. The past was beyond recapturing. She wanted to work hard and build a future for herself. She wanted to be free to make her own choices without worrying. She felt a flurry of anticipation when she passed a mileage marker—less than a hundred and fifty miles. Eureka!

Susan Tiffany Sullivan was thirty-two years old. She was considered tall at five feet, seven inches. Her completion had a country girl glow and her green eyes made contact with whomever she met with a frankness not usually seen in a young woman. The hair framing her face was a thick and curly auburn with golden highlights. She wore it just short enough to keep it under control. Her hairdresser of many years said Irish hair had a mind of its own, just like its hard-headed Irish owner. Susan didn't mind the hair or the playful stab at her personality. She had come from a people with a history of overcoming hardships by determination and hard work. Hardheaded meant obstinate. *She never thought of herself as obstinate, more like persevering and determined.*

Leaving her thriving catering business down in Florida was the hardest thing she'd ever done. The events of the past month seemed so surreal, she spoke aloud as if to confirm what was happening, "I loved my business and the people who worked for me." She wondered if they would find out she was gone first or receive the letter with the severance pay first. For a moment she wanted to cry, but that same spirit that had guided her through her mother's illness and college, and later helped her establish her own business would see her through what would be tough days ahead-and-.*she would soon have a thriving catering business in Georgia.*

When Susan was fifteen, her mom died of lymphoma. Those had been terrible days for a teenager trying to do the seemingly impossible task of establishing autonomy while being the obedient daughter. Her mom had been wonderful right up to the end, and that made it even worse. Who could she rail against when her hormones threatened to take over her body like the pods in the movie, *The Body Snatchers?*

Her dad, a civil engineer, understood thoroughly. He enrolled Susan in a Marshall Arts class that chewed her up and spit her out twice a week for six months. Susan had just enough energy left to accomplish her other obligations. The instructor had made Susan his protégée and subsequent prized student. The six years of ballet had prepared her well for the classes in Marshall Arts.

Susan's dad died when she was thirty. At that time, her catering business was already established. She was tripping along, enjoying her success—each day a challenge that only whet her desire for more success. She was not prepared for the overwhelming loss when her dad suddenly died of a heart attack. He had been a robust man all his life: A man of hard work and gusto. It just didn't connect in her over-simplified scheme of things, paired with his life credo of moderation. She had gone on with a fierce determination to outlast her grief. After she had found herself in her present dilemma, she remembered a Kenny Rogers song that sang, "You gotta know when to raise and know when to fold." That was her problem—she didn't know when to fold. A large percentage of books, songs, and poetry emphasize the fact that we don't often appreciate something until it's gone. That's true. We grow accustomed to having someone around and we simply don't realize how important he or she is to us. Sure, we say, "I love you," and mean it. But when we no longer have them—we realize how uncertain life is. Susan had been hit hard by her father's death when Tony Vascola entered the picture. He'd been lurking in his lair, observing her, before the death of her dad. She'd been too busy to notice. Tony's father, Giamo imagined himself to be a self-styled Godfather. He had started out as a tough on the docks of New York and then moved to SE Florida to wholesale vegetables. He built a flourishing business by every conceivable means of exploitation. He gradually branched out into more unsavory sidelines, until he became wealthy enough to feign respectability. The family ran a popular restaurant frequented by the wealthy, and when Susan's catering business took off, Giamo Vascola tried to buy it. Susan would not even consider his offers that eventually amounted to a sort of harassment. Finally Tony came around and approached her about allowing the restaurant to employ her catering service. She refused. For six months he was a constant thorn in her side until one night, after staying late at her business, some thugs tried to strong-arm her as she was going to her car. Normally one of her male staffers was there to protect her.

On this occasion, Toby, her protector for the night, had to go to the hospital due to a family emergency. The attack had escalated to the point that Susan was being held down on the pavement behind her shop by two tattooed, dirty youths while another was going through her purse looking for the key to her car. It was in her pocket. Tony appeared and routed them. She was bruised, skinned in areas, and so angry she wanted to go after the thugs. Tony talked her out of it, saying it might catch the attention of the press and give the area a bad name. That wouldn't be good for business. He was a perfect gentleman, insisting on following her home and waiting until he saw her lights go on before leaving. She saw him again in about two weeks at a party she was catering. Again, he was a perfect gentleman. When she ran into him again a month later, he asked if she would cater a private affair for him. He said his restaurant didn't have the type of gourmet food she specialized in. She agreed to look at her schedule and let him know.

Susan finally decided to cater for Tony, and had regretted it bitterly ever since. As she drove the last miles to her destination, she chided herself for leaving the CD in her Lincoln. It wasn't such a great novel, but it had kept her mind occupied by something other than the things that were flooding her mind now. The city limits sign was a welcome relief. There was some growth in the outskirts of town, but, hopefully, not enough to ruin the intimate setting she had loved. The sidewalks were extended all the way out to the edge of town and magnolias and crepe myrtles had been planted along the right of way. *Nice touch.* She found herself getting excited as she imagined she recognized some of the storefronts that had been there before. The first thing she needed to do was find a reasonably priced place to stay until her business took off. The drugstore up ahead might be a good place to get information. All she needed was a tiny apartment or room—just as long as it was as big as her car!

~2~

Susan was accustomed to turning heads—usually men's. As she walked into the drugstore, everyone's eyes were looking at her as if she were an apparition. She glanced in the mirror behind the cashier's back, wondering, *Have I overlooked something?* "Excuse me, I'm wondering if you can give me some information," she asked. At that point, conversation at the old-fashioned soda fountain counter came to a standstill. It had been a long and nerve-racking night. She felt almost giddy with fatigue. Resisting the urge to laugh as the cashier stood there staring without saying a word., Susan continued, "I'm wondering if you can tell me if anyone rents rooms in town?" The cashier seemed to regain her speech as she said, "Go down three blocks to the library. Mrs. Martin can tell you anything you wanta know." Susan thanked her and left. She could hear conversation buzzing as the door closed behind her. *Give them time. Right now I'm a stranger!*

The library was evidently new. The grounds were spacious, providing benches for people under trees spaced, not by nature, but an architect. The building was a combination of stone and brick. Large windows shared a duel function of letting in light as well as showing the beauty of azaleas and lilies growing in well-designed groupings outside. Her dad had always said you could judge a town by its library. When she went in the door, there was a middle-age woman at the checkout desk. Susan approached her and asked, "Mrs. Martin?" The woman looked up at Susan with a vacant, confused expression. “No, Mrs. Martin’s in her office. The second door on the right.” Susan walked to the second door. The upper portion had glass and Susan could see a woman with short, silver hair sitting at a desk, working on a computer. Before Susan could knock, the woman looked up and motioned for Susan to come in, then stood smiling as she commented, “I hope you’re my new volunteer.” Susan liked the woman instantly.

Mrs. Martin was of medium height and somewhere in her sixties. Her pleasant face had the kind of wrinkles left behind by many years of smiling, not frowning. She was the kind of woman you instinctively wanted to please. “No, I’m sorry,” Susan replied, “I was told you might know someone with a room I could rent.” Mrs. Martin leaned over, extending her hand, “I’m Julia Martin,” she said, taking Susan’s hand. “Susan Sullivan,” Susan replied. Mrs. Martin’s handshake brought an instant epitome to mind: *Steel* magnolia. She didn’t shake hands like a dead fish or give a fingertip excuse for a handshake. “Have a seat, Susan, and let me think a minute. Do you have any bad habits, like smoking or such?” Susan was both amused and puzzled. “I don’t smoke, but I’m not sure what else you consider to be a bad habit. I do use alcohol in moderation, which I consider a choice, not a habit. Mrs. Martin continued to look at Susan, as if assessing her, then asked, “Tell me about yourself, your plans.”

It was Susan’s time to ponder over her position. She liked this woman. What she was asking was a reasonable request. This wasn’t like her former situation where she was having her life put under a microscope. “I’m planning on opening a catering business. I have limited funds and need to cut expenses as much as possible. Since I’ll be working so much, I won’t require much more than a bed and bath.” Mrs. Martin smiled as she said, “Well, my dear, I know the ideal place for you to stay: My home. It’s down the street about four blocks. The number is four one five.” Susan was simultaneously pleased and dubious. No! *This is too easy!* She had envisioned some back street little house with a widow renting out a room to make ends meet, not *this*. “How much?” Susan inquired. “Oooh, would fifty dollars a week fit your budget?” Mrs. Martin asked. “Mrs. Martin, I think that would be more than reasonable,” Susan replied. “Very well, I’ll meet you there in about an hour,” Mrs. Martin said as she stood up, again extending her hand. “It’s the large white frame, number four one five.” Susan had been pleasantly dismissed. Susan shook her new landlady’s hand and left, wondering as if she had just met the equivalent of her fairy god mother—or someone out of a Stephen King novel.

Susan hadn’t eaten since the previous afternoon. Hungry, she drove to a small inviting café she had passed earlier. The restaurant owner’s goodwill was essential to her success, so she needed to introduce herself. Glancing at her Daily Planner, she saw his name. Thank God she had had enough presence of mind to research Martinsville's restaurants on the internet back at West Palm Beach's library. She knew she had to leave her PC behind, so she avoided putting anything on it that would lead Tony to her.

There were only a few people in Metcalf's café as she entered. The stares were accepted as a small-town characteristic—along with warmth, friendliness, and trustworthiness. They tended to be suspicious of newcomers, a quality she respected. The menu was pretty standard and the food acceptable. There was a newspaper left from an earlier breakfast patron. Reading it, while she waited for her food to be served, the idea of being able to keep up with the people in an entire town was refreshing. This was going to be her town, and the people she was reading about were going to be her neighbors, her friends, her patrons. She would remember the good, and if she couldn't forget the bad, at least she had learned. By the time she had read the paper and eaten her lunch, it was time to meet Mrs. Martin. As she was leaving, she introduced herself to the owner.

When she arrived at 415 Main Street, there was a car in the drive, hopefully Mrs. Martin's. Most men wouldn't tolerate having a paying guest in their home, so she assumed there wasn't a Mr. Martin, especially under the circumstances. *You can't read character by talking to a person for thirty minutes!* The house was a large white sprawling ante bellum with columns across the front and a wrap-around porch. A beautiful old door with a cut-glass oval insert and cut-glass sidelights on either side graced the entryway. On either side of the wide steps there were large Grecian urns with ivy and geraniums cascading from them. When Susan walked to the front door, Mrs. Martin opened the door and said,. "Welcome to the Martin home, Susan."

Susan was reminded of the tours she had taken in the historic homes of Washington, D.C. and Williamsburg. And, in fact, that's exactly what Julia Martin did! As she walked Susan through the house, she told about the house, both its place in the history of the Martin family and the Confederacy. As she talked, it was evident she was proud of both the heritage of her husband's family and her own. There was nothing pretentious in her manner, rather she was relating something she considered to be sacred—the family honor. *We are people of honor and trustworthiness; we expect the same of you.* Subtle!

After the tour was over, Mrs. Martin invited Susan into the kitchen for a glass of iced tea. Julia Martin's openness and hospitality affected Susan like a hypnotic drug. When the conversation ended, Susan was amazed at the amount of information Julia—she insisted that Susan refer to her by her given name—had obtained about *her* history. Susan offered to pay Mrs. Martin in cash, but was persuaded to wait until she had a bank account established to finalize their tenant relationship. It took Susan two hours to move things from the car to her room. Afterwards she showered and debated taking a quick nap, but hearing faint sounds of pots and pans, together with a wonderful aroma signaling the cooking of food, vetoed the nap. She was too much of a culinary artist to forgo seeing food being prepared, so she made her way to the kitchen where she found Julia attired in an apron, and as much in command as she had been at her library desk. Whatever she was cooking smelled wonderful. "Come in dear," Julia urged, "Feel free to have the run of the house." Susan laughed and asked, "Julia, how do you know I'm not a female Ted Bundy or some other diabolical psycho?" Julia turned and gave Susan a piercing look and retorted, "Susan, I am a Prescott. We have the ability to judge a person's character. Don't ever assume that I'm a sentimental old woman. I'm not."

Susan had meant to be playfully candid, but quickly apologized when she realized she had inadvertently insulted Julia. "I'm sorry, Julia. I'm . . . . overwhelmed. I've never met anyone like you before. I'm humbled and gratified that you have so much confidence in me. I promise . . . I'll never make you regret it." At this moment the phone rang. When Julia got off the line, she asked Susan if she would mind watching the stove and making a salad, with the explanation, "Velma Reese next door has a husband with Alzheimer's. Henry has gone on a rampage again. Seems I'm the only one who can talk him down. Sad, sad situation. I'll be back as soon as possible."

Susan had made the salad and was standing at the stove when she heard a door close. Assuming it was Julia, Susan continued removing the pools of fat that had accumulated in the marvelous sauce Julia had concocted. As she concentrated on this, a very sonorous male voice asked, "What do we have here? Could it be possible that my mother has finally given up cooking and hired a beautiful cook?" Susan turned and faced the speaker. He was medium height, medium age, and medium weight. But thereafter, any sign of mediumness was absent. This man had thick dark hair and the most piercing green eyes under heavy black lashes and brows set in a warrior's face that might have graced a Roman statue. He had just a hint of a five o'clock shadow and the color of skin that would soon turn bronze in the sun. He was handsome in an extremely masculine way. Even his playful words warned that he was not to be taken lightly. No pretty boy, but a man for sure! Excitement and curiosity broached the question, *Who was he?*

~3~

Susan was not the type of person who was easily rattled or usually at a loss for words. But she stood there for a moment, as though dumbstruck. The quizzical, slightly amused look on this man's face did not help. The long night of driving without sleep had left her feeling slightly light-headed. "Well?" he asked, raising his eyebrows. The gesture was an indication that he was accustomed to receiving an immediate response to a question. Words flashed through Susan's mind . . . . *not husband, not brother, must be son.* Finally recovering her composure, she extended her hand (unfortunately, the one with the spoon) and said, "I'm Susan Sullivan, your . . . uh, uh . . . ." "Dream?" he suggested. *The man was flirting with her outrageously and playing with her like a cat with a mouse!*. With a soft laugh, he took the spoon from her hand laid it on the stove then encompassing her hand in both of his he gently pressed it as he said, "Jason Martin, I live here."

When Susan finally answered, she tried to modulate her voice in such a way that this arrogant man would not be alienated but quietly put in his place. Extricating her hand, she laughed and said, "I'm sure that finding a strange woman in your kitchen must be disconcerting, at the least. I'm afraid neither of us were prepared." Jason Martin tipped his head forward, indicating for her to continue. Susan's Irish was aroused by his dominant manner but realizing her tentative position, she acquiesced. "When your mother makes up her mind about something, she doesn't hesitate to move ahead. I'll be a guest in your home for a while." Jason Martin was totally undaunted. Instead of backing away, he dipped the spoon he had taken from her into the sauce, tasted it, then giving the spoon back to her, he said, "I can see why my mother made such a decision. You're very perceptive, beautiful, and—by the taste of that sauce-a good cook. In fact, if you'll be staying here for any length of time, I may need to start jogging an extra mile. His eyes were locked on hers as he continued, "I love good food almost as much as I love beautiful women."

Julia's entrance rescued Susan. "Susan, I am so sorry to leave you without first warning you of my wayward son." A little breathless, Julia turned to Jay. "I hope you introduced yourself to Susan?" The idea of a mother talking to her mature son in such a way prepared Susan for the worst. Instead of bristling, however, Jason walked over to Julia and kissed her on the cheek, and, with an obviously suppressed smile, retorted, "Yes mother, Susan and I are now acquainted."

"Well dear," Julia said in an exasperated voice, "Poor Velma called me just as I was preparing dinner and said Henry had gone berserk again, so I had to run off and leave Susan to tend everything and make the salad." Jay's eyebrows—God, they were so dark and thick and *gorgeous*-went up again, as he turned to Susan. Then, before she could turn away-*he winked!* Susan felt the flush in her face and turned toward Julia. "Would you like for me to set the table?" she asked. Julia's answer was spontaneous. "Dear Susan, you are going to be an absolute pleasure to have around. Jay, help Susan set the table while I finish in here."

"So," he asked as they went into the dining room, "*Can* you cook?" "Yes, as a matter of fact, I can," Susan replied. "If given the opportunity, I would have told you I didn't prepare the sauce." "All right, all right," he countered," I shall add "honest" to your aforementioned attributes. Let's set the table and then we're going to sit down and have a nice glass of wine—if that suits you. And, please call me Jay." At that moment Susan wasn't sure what she wanted to call this man, but it wasn't anything as polite as Jason or Jay. But she managed in her most cordial voice, "Yes, that would be nice," as she carefully avoided eye contact. Her normal poise was replaced with a feeling of girlish naiveté and irritation. She needed something more than silverware to concentrate on. This man was arrogant—and admittedly—arousing, and *fascinating!*

By the time Julia, Jay and Susan had settled down in the living room with their wine, Susan had regained her composure and felt prepared for Jay's verbal jousting.

"So tell me Susan, what brings you to a provincial little town like Martinsville?" Susan told Jay of traveling through the town years before with her father and how they had both loved the clean, quaint, times-past ambiance of the area. "What do you plan to do here?" was his next question. Before she could answer, Julia interrupted, "Susan, you'll have to overlook Jay's interrogative manner. He's an attorney. It's hard for him to revert back to normal, gracious conversation after being in court all day." The remark was made in the most pleasant of voices, with just a tiny bit of humor. Jay smiled his half smile and said, "My mother seems to think that my manner is a little brusque. I apologize if that's so." "No apology is necessary," Susan replied. "I really would prefer that you be yourself, or whatever you're comfortable with." Julia spoke up again. "Jay probably remains the most eligible bachelor in town because of his courtroom manner." Jay laughed and quipped, looking at Julia, "That remark was an oxymoron. You're saying that no one will have me because of my manners, and yet I'm still being pursued." Then, turning to Susan, he remarked, "My mother is concerned that I won't marry and have children to carry on the family name. I've assured her if I don't marry by my fortieth birthday, I'll marry Agnes Smith who works at the library. Now Susan, back to my question."

But Susan was again irritated, "And what does Agnes Smith have to say about that?" Jay was obviously pleased that Susan had taken the bait. "Agnes Smith is my former first grade teacher and says if my mother insists that I marry, she will do me the honor." Susan was end-played, so ignored Jay's little joke by answering his question, "I'm a caterer. I've gotten tired of the big-city life and want to live in a small town, remembered Martinsville, so here I am." Jay was not through. "Veni, vidi, vici," he quipped. Now Susan's Irish was really up. *Forget fascinating—this man was infuriating!* Susan took a deep breath before answering in a pleasant tone, "You flatter me, but I don't think you can compare me to Caesar." Susan saw just a hint of surprise—or was it amusement—on Jay's face before he uttered, "Ooooh, the lady knows Latin." Susan wondered *what have I gotten myself into?*

During this exchange, Julia had left the room and now reappeared with the announcement, "Dinner is served." When they went into the dining room, Jay pulled out Susan's chair, and after seating her, went around to where his mother was serving the plates and seated her. Good manners were obviously ingrained. *Was this a mother's boy?* Susan had visions of an adolescent Jay putting a frog down a girl's neck. After Jay had seated

Julia, he leaned close to her ear and said, so low that Susan barely caught it, "You're wonderful."

The meal was delicious. Julia was an excellent cook. Both Julia and Jay were surprised and pleased to find capers in their salad. Susan felt a little foolish listening to Julia's and Jay's murmuring compliments. She was accustomed to having people like her food, but other's praise had never seemed this personal. She was embarrassed. She had been reared on the ideal of striving for excellence, and compliments were almost extraneous especially coming from Jay after his rude behavior. She turned the conversation by asking Julia about the ingredients in her marinara sauce. From there the conversation became more relaxed, with information exchanged that would help Susan launch her business. Also, there was a social coming up at the country club on the weekend and Susan was invited. Apparently Jay escorted Julia to various events, and it would be a threesome. Finally, Jay excused himself, saying he had a Kiwanis meeting to attend, but suggested that he would be available the following evening to show Susan around town. Susan felt the tension in her neck as she thought *I believe I'm going to be sick tomorrow night with a terrible headache.*

After Julia and Susan cleared the table and began cleaning up the kitchen, Julia, asking Susan about the time-frame involved in setting up her professional work-place, offered the use of her kitchen until the professional one was ready. Susan was delighted and overwhelmed with this woman's generosity. Julia's kitchen had limitations, but she would be able to handle some simple affairs. *This was what she needed—to be able to throw herself into her work!* Susan's ever-present independent nature was having a battle with Susan's ever-present industrious nature. She was now living in the Martin's home, and evidently expected to share their food. She did not really know Julia and Jay. Were things moving too fast? Was she going to become included in someone else's agenda? Julia seemed wonderful. And Jay? He simultaneously intrigued and upset her. She had just gotten away from one unpleasant affair. Once, in college, when she was in a similar dilemma, her father told her, "Don't jump from the frying pan into the fire."

Her silence must have made Julia wonder, for she asked, "A penny for your thoughts?" The uncertainty must have shown in Susan's eyes, as she turned and faced Julia. To say what she felt was necessary, but *please Dear God, help me to say the right thing.* Before she could even utter a word, Julia Martin walked over, and putting her hand on Susan's arm, said, "What a strange woman you must think I am, Susan Sullivan. I have taken you in and am offering you the run of my house. But I'm not worried about you and I don't want you to worry about me. Look at me. I am sixty-six years old. I have a Masters Degree in English. I was the first female on the board of directors at the First National Bank. I am personally responsible for contributing over two thousand of the reference books in our library. I have been to every worthwhile place to see on this earth, I come from revered ancestors and had a wonderful marriage to a man with similar credentials. But everything I have done or become in life is tied to people. To be a better librarian, to improve banking by giving a woman's input, and to better understand people in other lands. It seems on the surface to smack of a privileged lady collecting her laurels—*noblesse oblige. Not so.* I was taught that the most important thing a person does in his life pales in comparison with the relationships he establishes with people. I have a wonderful son to carry on his father's name, but I am not ready to throw in the towel yet! You are the most exciting, authentic person I have met in so long that I had forgotten what it was like to meet such a person. It's almost like being young again. So please, allow me to help you."

Susan wanted to put her arms around this wonderful woman and give her a big hug. But instead, she just said, "Julia, I can't tell you how much I appreciate your generosity. You're like having a second mother." Julia Martin had no such qualms about displaying her feelings. She hugged Susan, saying, "Susan, I know integrity when I see it, and I'm a dyed-in-the-wool mother. You just concentrate on your catering business and let me do some mothering. Okay?" All in all, it had been quite a day!

~4~

Tuesday morning found Susan up at six-thirty. For some reason, she didn't want Jay to see her out jogging. She couldn't figure out which was worse in her mind—afraid that Jay would see her or disgusted with herself for being afraid that Jay would see her. As she took off running down the sidewalk, the paper boy threw the paper up on the Martin's porch. He was about sixteen years of age, and was watching her so intently that he undoubtedly ran afoul of the next door neighbor's gate post. Hearing a noise and a muffled sound of pain, she turned around to see him sprawled on the ground. She turned back around quickly, hoping he hadn't seen her looking. His dignity had taken a bad enough blow as it was, not to mention his body. She had her odometer attached to her wrist and had decided to run an adventurous route. She wanted to be disciplined, but not a slave to discipline. Life was meant to be a joy, not pursued like a catechism. The air was still cool and crisp for late April. In Florida, she would have been sweaty already. As she ran she saw an odd looking man watching birds in a nest. There were other signs of activity as people prepared to meet the demands of the day. *This is now my town!*

The run was a good one. She had covered a little less than her goal, but the early morning air made her feel alive and she enjoyed seeing the houses without having to worry about driving. Just as she entered the foyer, Jay walked out of his bedroom. He had on a pair of running shorts and a sheepish look on his face. Susan wasn't sure if she should pause and speak to him, or just say a quick "hi" in passing. So, as she walked past him, she simply said in a low voice, "Enjoy your run. It's a great day." His reply was sort of a "Humpha." Apparently, he was not a morning person. *Another reason to avoid the man, she told herself. I am definitely a morning person.* Susan thought of the remark Jay had made about running an extra mile. *Does he run routinely?* Before she could retreat to her room, Julia appeared. "Good morning, Susan," she said with enthusiasm. *This was the hallmark of a morning person.* "Help yourself to whatever you usually eat. I'm going out and spray the aphids on my roses before I dress for work. Oh. And there's coffee already brewed. Jay usually drinks only one cup, so help yourself." She had turned and was out sight before Susan could say no more than "Thanks." What a dynamo. Julia Martin was the most incredible woman Susan had ever met. When she thought of the accomplishments Julia had achieved, she was awed. *If only I have achieved a fraction of such by the time I'm her age!*

By noon, Susan had opened an account at the First National Bank and looked at six potential sites for her business. The one she finally decided upon was moderately priced and centrally located. The owner had also offered some perks, such as starting out with a lower rent, then increasing it later after her business had a chance to take off. He also offered her a rider on his insurance on the building. The fact that she was staying at the Martin's probably had more clout than her independent Irish nature would care to admit. She thought of her dad and what he would think. He had always advised her to pick her friends well, saying, "Good friends are better than money in the bank." Her dad would approve of the Martins. She pondered the fact that she had used the plural. *Okay, I admit there is a certain confidence and attraction that I feel for Jay. But sharks also fascinate me.* Before her thoughts could leap into some areas she had rather not explore, she forced herself to concentrate on the next necessary step, ordering equipment.

When she got back to the Martin home, Julia's car was parked judiciously in front of the house, leaving the driveway for Susan. As she opened the front door into the foyer, Julia called from the kitchen, "Susan dear, I've made a large chef's salad. Please help yourself if you're hungry." Susan thought of one of the times she and her dad had gone swimming at the beach. The tide was rolling in with big swells and Susan had tried to fight the water. Her dad convinced her to surrender herself to the tide. It had started out as a sort of man against nature, and nature had been winning. Now Julia *was* mother nature. Susan had to surrender. "Julia, thank you. It sounds wonderful."

They spent their lunch discussing what Susan had thus far accomplished. Julia approved of Susan's choice of the Beech street location for her shop and was amazed at the deal that Ralph Getz had cut her. "Susan," she remarked with surprise, "No one can squeeze a deal like that out of Ralph." "Don't tell me that, Julia," Susan replied. "I keep waiting for something to come crashing down. Either that or I'm going to wake up and find out that I'm dreaming."

Susan's afternoon was equally busy as she bought a computer, printer, fax machine, and a cell phone. After a phone was installed, she signed up for an internet provider. She had zipped her through a process in an hour that usually took several days. By five o'clock she was ordering equipment on the internet. And by six o'clock she was in the foyer of the Martin home.

This time Julia did not greet her. Instead, Jay met her and offered her a glass of wine. She started to decline, remembering his invitation to take her around town tonight and her decision to feign a headache. She surprised herself by accepting the glass of wine which he served after guiding her to the sun room on the back of the house. There was a CD playing that was a collection of old RB favorites. "Want something to nibble on while you're drinking that?" he asked as he handed her the glass of wine. *Where was that outrageous man of last night?* Again, she was tempted to decline, but instead, said, "Thank you, that would be great." When he came back, he brought smoked oysters, shrimp dip, crackers, and a tomato cocktail sauce that was guaranteed to open your sinuses and thrill your palette. He asked about her day and listened as she related what had gone on. Before she could protest, he had refilled her wine glass. It was one of the most delicious pinot blanc she had ever drank. She had not realized how hungry she was as she started on the shrimp and oysters. When she took the last cracker, Jay was filling her wine glass again. It tasted too good, and she was feeling too relaxed to protest.

By the time Susan was half finished with her third glass of wine, Julia came in. It seems that Julia was the favorite pitch-hitter for anyone with problems. One of the members of her church had undergone surgery and Julia had not only cooked the family a meal, she had gone over and served it, and then cleaned up afterward. *Not ready to throw in the towel*, indeed! Julia was going to wring it out and mop up the whole town! However, even though she looked a little tired, she inquired as to whether or not Susan and Jay had eaten. "Just enough to help me tolerate three glasses of wine," Susan told her. Julia cut her eyes over at Jay, who promptly defended himself. "Julia, you have always said that there were occasionally three-drink days. I decided today was one for Susan." "Well," declared Julia, "I haven't had a three-drink day, but I would appreciate you fetching me a glass of wine. Is that from the case we had shipped recently?" Jay's smile and nod affirmed this. He stood up, picked up the empty bottle and left. Julia walked over to Susan, patted her on the shoulder and said, "I think you and Jay should wait another night for touring the town. You look as though you are slightly blitzed."

"Oh no you don't, you interfering old hussy," Jay said in a mock chiding voice as he came back into the room. "Susan needs to be slightly inebriated for the grand tour. And it took the finest wine we had to get her there." Susan leaned back and marveled at the interplay between mother and son. Could there possibly be a few more strings in Jay's bow than she imagined? He was definitely an enigma. She looked up after finishing the last of her wine. Jay had stood and walked over and asked as he held up his hand, "How many fingers do you see? Having given the correct answer, they left. The ride through town gave a whole new meaning to buildings and landmarks. Jay knew the history of not only the more famous residents of Martinsville, he could also told anecdotes about ordinary folks whose ancestors still resided in Martinsville. After thirty minutes of history, Susan understood a lot more about the town that she was planning to spend the rest of her life in, but she also knew more about the man conducting the tour. Last night he had struck her as an abrasive, arrogant snob. Tonight he was knowledgeable, well mannered, and, at times, funny. They passed the man she had seen bird-watching earlier. "Who is he?" she asked.

"Tom Jeter is our town eccentric. Fine man. My former Scout leader who took all the scouts camping. Taught us about the outdoors, birds in particular. He wasn't too much older than us. Sad tale, married for a while until his wife ran off with someone from the county fair. He was pretty bad off for a while. Seems very content now."

When they had covered the greater part of the town, they passed a Dairy Queen and Jay pulled in. Susan said nothing as he pulled up to the drive-in window and ordered two coffees with ice cream in them. When the coffees were ready, he handed her one and drove one-handed over to a spot that was on a slight elevation, and in the distance they could see the court house, a traditional marble building with Greek columns. There were flood lights shining on the building that gave it an almost ethereal appearance. "That building was commissioned by my great grandfather, Elijah Prescott, and survived the Civil War. It's not just a beautiful building, it represents my heritage, both as a Prescott and as an American fortunate enough to be born in this country. Was your father in the armed services during a war?

The question was unexpected and Susan wondered where *this* was going. Jay immediately apologized, "I'm sorry, I didn't mean to pry." Susan knew he had read the wrong thing in her hesitation. "No, no. I don't think you're prying, it's just something my dad didn't like to talk about. He was a prisoner during the Korean War and I think they almost broke his spirit. It was a very painful experience."

Jay said nothing. Susan wondered if he was a little embarrassed that he might have seemed to be bragging about his family and then wondered about hers. Susan didn't say anything for a few minutes. The two just sat there in silence. Finally, she said, "I understand what you're talking about. It may seem corny to some people, but when I hear *America The Beautiful*, I feel teary eyed. We live in a great country."

Jay started the car and drove home. As they walked up the front walkway, Susan thanked Jay for the evening. When they were in the foyer, before Susan realized what was happening, he took her by the shoulders as if to kiss her, then softly murmured, "Goodnight," before turning and walking to his room, closing the door. She stood in the hall for a moment, stunned. Then as she went to her room she remembered what her dad had told her. All she could think of was, *I've jumped, Dad, and the fire is hot!"*

~5~

As Pinkie drove into Martinsville, he had the same sensation he felt when he was forced to stay in the sun too long. This was a small town—a stranger was bound to be spotted—and Pinkie's role called for anonymity. Pinkie was called by this nickname because of his skin color. He was not an albino but had less pigmentation in his skin than was normal. As a youth growing up in Florida, he had to learn at an early age to avoid the sun or get blistered. He had not been happy going to public school. The kids sensed the difference in his skin color and tended to leave him out of things. By the time he hit teenage, he dropped out of school and sundown had become the beginning of his day. He hung around the pool parlor and eventually was *chosen* for his various talents to do odd jobs for the owner. Later on, he was introduced to a member of the local mob and became an invaluable asset of the lower echelon crime boss. From then on, although he avoided jail time, his vocation was crime. Pinkie had the equivalent of a ninth grade education but the talent of looking like someone who was formerly on the basketball team in high school and was now selling insurance or some other such occupation. His role as a seasoned criminal had hardened the odd unhappy boy of grade school into a self-confident brute of a man not to be messed with. He made up for his lack of height by his stocky body. His hair was light and his skin color was now a nondescript fleshy look that bordered on ruddy because of his daily consumption of above average amounts of alcohol. He was neither attractive nor particularly ugly. At five feet ten inches and weighing one hundred ninety pounds, Pinkie was a perfect *John Doe;* a nameless entity. And therein lay part of his value as a member of the underworld. The other element that made him an asset to the mob was his cunning. He had the instincts of an animal, and when stalking a prey, he could strike at just the right moment, eliminating his victim. The one distinguishing feature that Pinkie had was his pleasant voice, although he didn't talk much. Had his fate been different, he might have been a radio announcer. Unfortunately, the thing that he most prided himself in, and what had kept him from serving jail time, was his ability with his hands. He could break a man's neck without the victim making a sound. The fact that he didn't need to carry a gun made it difficult for the police to link him to a crime.

When Pinkie reached Martinsville, the first thing he did was rent a room at an older motel called Days Rest. The motel had been around a long time and was no longer on the list of better motels. It rented mostly to truck drivers and month to month lessees, and was in a less desirable part of town and that made his comings and goings of little interest to people caught up in the daily struggle to survive until the next pay check or welfare check. Once he settled into the motel room, Pinkie felt a little more comfortable.

Several blocks away, on Thursday morning after her jog, Susan dressed and went to her shop to meet a building contractor. Julia had wisely told Susan that she would probably choose Frank Nigel after getting three estimates; but if you didn't get estimates from several people, there was usually talk of favoritism, and Julia didn't want the town's people to think her unfair. In his youth, Frank had worked on some of John Portman's projects and later decided a small town life was better than making a lot of money and not having roots. He was sitting outside her shop in his truck when Susan drove up.

Frank watched Susan unlock the door, then unfolded his six foot four frame out of his truck and walked over, standing back just a little in case she might be spooked. Frank's knowledge of women was inverse to his knowledge of building, and that was prodigious. Just in case Susan hadn't seen him, Frank cleared his throat before speaking. "Ms. Sullivan, I'm Frank Nigel." Susan didn't turn around and face Frank until she had gotten inside the door. His voice sounded like it had run through a hollow tube and Susan liked him, sight unseen. When she did turn and face him, she was surprised that such a tall, almost skinny man had such a deep voice.

He thrust out his hand and shook hers, saying, “I’m glad to be of help to anyone that has Julia’s stamp of approval.” His mouth never changed but his eyes expressed a friendly expression as well as any smile might.

Susan was still not accustomed to so many doors being opened for her, and was momentarily caught off balance. She managed to say, “Thanks a lot, Frank. Julia has been very generous. A great lady.” Susan had a folder of brochures in one hand and looked around for a place to lay it that was dust free. *No such luck.* “Let me show you what I need so you can give me some feedback.” With that remark, she guided Frank through her list of equipment placement and the necessary structural changes she had in mind. He did very little talking, just occasionally asking a question. Less than an hour later, he guided her back through her requests and suggested a plan he thought would serve her needs. Susan had never worked with anyone so quick to absorb ideas. He told her he would need a couple of days to draw up the plan and check on current prices, then before leaving made an appointment for one of his men to come back and take measurements.

Susan hated to call anyone else, knowing she would ultimately hire Frank Nigel for the job; but she also knew she had to follow Julia’s advice, not for any other reason other than her reliance on Julia’s wisdom. She called the second contractor and made an appointment for him to come by late in the afternoon when she knew Frank’s assistant would be gone. Meanwhile, she drove several blocks to a hardware store and picked up some cleaning supplies. The workmen would soon have sawdust and the usual trimmings all over the place, but right now the dust was starting to get her down.

Two hours later she had managed to accumulate a pile of dust and assorted trash in a pile in the center of the room, when behind her that familiar quasi-serious-sexual voice asked. “Do you do offices?” Susan turned to face Jay and wondered if he knew the effect he had on her. He had that same half-smile on his face that both excited and irritated her. She had pulled her hair back in a ponytail but a few stray curls hung down and were sticking to her face from the perspiration. “No, but I could certainly use some help here!” Jay’s laugh reminded Susan of the arrogance he had previously shone, leaving her feeling foolish and ready to do battle! Then, his voice took on a more solicitous tone, “I have to be back in court in an hour and thought you might be too busy to go out for lunch. Come sit in the car and eat a deli sandwich with me.” The look on Susan’s face must have revealed her feelings of ambiguity. “You do like roast beef?” he asked. “Thank you, that’s very thoughtful of you. Give me a minute to get cleaned up," she answered, hoping her voice didn't reveal the roller coaster ride her emotions were on.

When she returned from the restroom, Jay was talking to a young man who was apparently Frank Nigel's assistant. "Here's Ms. Sullivan now," Jay said, as Susan walked up to the two men. "Susan, this is Mike James, Frank's right hand man." The young man wiped his hand on the side of his jeans as Susan offered her hand. His "Nice to meet you Ma'am," was pure southern dialect as it rolled out, and his smile was the kind that made you glad he was there as it stretched his mouth open, revealing a large set of teeth that gleamed with a well-scrubbed look. With this young man as a bonus, Frank Nigel was as good as hired. "I'll be about forty-five minutes if you want to go out for something," he said, pulling his digital measure out. As Susan turned, Jay already had the door open for her and walked around his car and opened the passenger door. On the front seat was a bag from Davinci Deli. "Our drinks are on the floor, so watch it," he told her, "I assume you drink tea." "My favorite drink, excluding water," she quietly said. "We could go to the park if you like," he suggested. "No, I think I need to stick around just in case," she demurred. *Our conversation is like two cautious tennis players, lobbing the ball back and forth,* she thought. "So, do I detect a note of displeasure in my idea of a luncheon?" he asked. Suddenly Susan caught on. *This man really likes me!* "No, no," she objected, "I think when I saw you with your suit and impeccably starched shirt, I felt very grungy. This is so very sweet and thoughtful of you." Something suddenly occurred to her. She stopped unwrapping the sandwich and hesitated before she asked him, "Was this Julia's idea?"

One of those heavy black eyebrows went up as he asked, "Do you really imagine that my mother is still directing my life?" Embarrassed, Susan continued unwrapping the sandwich. "No, she replied. "You're absolutely the last person I would expect to have *any* woman directing."

"Well," he said, "Don't tell that to the judge sitting on the bench today. I walk on egg-shells when I'm in her court." Susan asked, "Are you telling me that in a small town like Martinsville, you actually have a female judge?"

"All two hundred pounds of her," he quipped.

"Is her expertise as big as her body?" Susan asked.

His answer denoted his respect for the judge. "Suffice it to say that every weekend while her more petit sisters were out dating, she was burning the midnight oil and memorizing law books. She's earned her right to sit on the bench. I shouldn't have said anything about her size. I was being a bore."

He was looking at Susan as if for absolution. “Perhaps her size was only incidental to her success,” Susan stated. “She may have preferred to study instead of dating. If what your mother says is true about your popularity with the females of this town, maybe her weight was more to your advantage than hers.” “Exactly what are you suggesting?” Jay asked. “Well,” Susan replied, “How would you feel about facing her in court if she were one of your former girlfriends?” “Unnnh,” Jay winced, “You’ve got a point there. But don’t lend a lot of credence to Julia’s opinion concerning my popularity with the women. After all, she is my mother, and rather prejudiced in regard to me. Anyway, we need to finish our lunch and get back to work. It looks like Mike is about ready to wind it up in there.”

After Susan had thanked Jay for the lunch and he left, she couldn’t help but feel a certain satisfaction in knowing that the judge was overweight. The idea that she was satisfied irritated her. *I should feel ashamed, so why aren’t I?*

~6~

In the neighborhood where Pinkie had taken up temporary residence, it didn't take long for him to ferret out the transients who were stranded in the town and would do just about anything for a few bucks to get them out, or buy a little something to help them forget where they were. The sort of information that Pinkie was buying was innocuous enough to keep him from tangling with the law, but important enough to help him achieve his directive. His boss had been resolute-the woman was not be harmed! Pinkie hated this kind of assignment. He'd prefer a quick kill any day. In and out in a hurry was his credo. He wondered if the boss realized how hard it was to get reliable information in a small town like this. Pinkie was supposed to gather as much information as possible in order to jettison her plans, and then what—force her back to West Palm Beach? If she spent all her money, and then something happened to her . . . *never mind that kind of thinking.* He'd be better off in a jail than have to face the mob. He'd managed to find out that she had rented a building a few blocks over. He had driven by the address, but needed to wait until dark when he wouldn't attract attention casing the place. Maybe he could get into the building tonight, or at least find an entry. He usually ate only two meals a day; at ten in the morning and then about nine at night. It was now three thirty, and he had another three hours before he could work. He pulled his fifth of Scotch out of the drawer and poured about three fingers worth in the glass he had found in the bathroom. The glass was cloudy. Cripes! This was what he hated about this kind of job. You had to deal with the low-life! One nice thing about a good strong proof, it sterilized as good as wood alcohol. Pinkie lay down and propped on a couple of pillows on the bed and watched a soap opera with the sound off. By the time he finished his Scotch, he'd be gone to la la land.

While Pinkie was getting pleasantly inebriated, several blocks away, Susan was painfully going through an interview with the second contractor, Jack Paine. When Susan saw Jack, she was grateful she had finished sweeping the trash up and had carried it out.

Jack Paine had on a pair of clean starched blue jeans that looked as though they would remain standing after he stepped out of them. Susan felt dishonest just having him there and tried to ease her conscience by reminding herself mentally that the man might redeem himself at any moment. It didn't happen. When he left after forty-five minutes spent at miscommunications and cross-purposes, his jeans were still impeccably clean, and Susan was perspiring. Not improving the situation, Ralph Getz dropped by to see how things were going. He was a nice enough man, but she had had a grueling day and he seemed antsy about letting anyone in to the other half of the building. Apparently, When the building was built years ago, it was intended to be one unit, and now there had to be a change in the electrical system. Getz was asking her to be responsible for the key being returned to him each day that the electrical work was going on. In addition, someone referred by Julia had called right after Frank Nigel's assistant, Mike, had left, wanting her to cater an affair. Julia had already told people of her catering services and with everything combined, she was feeling the pressure. As soon as she'd gotten off the phone with her new client, Jack Paine had walked in. To top the day, Ralph Getz came in and made his ridiculous request, and wanting to get rid of him, she agreed, then immediately regretted it after he'd left. Susan sat down on a crate she'd found in the back and picked up her flat soda she'd *gotten too busy to drink,* taking a swallow as she looked at her watch. Seven o'clock! No wonder she was so tired. In fact, if she had not been so tired, she might have noticed the car parked across the street with the man who had been watching her shop for the past fifteen minutes.

Pinkie had been watching Susan, but he'd also been watching for any signs of regular scheduled police activity. *In a small burg like this, what's to steal?* But, as if in answer to his question, a patrol car pulled up and parked behind Susan's Maxima. Pinkie waited about three minutes for the officer to go inside before he pulled away. He didn't have any respect for the law in general, and he considered the law in a small town as a notch below Barney Fife in the Mayberry sit com. Air heads. As he drove away, Pinkie decided to take an early dinner since he wasn't sure how long the job tonight would take. There was a roadhouse out off the interstate, He could eat and be back by eight or nine. By that time the woman would be gone, and the cop would be somewhere else and wouldn't bother checking this area again. As Pinkie drove away, he had formed a plan for later and knew just exactly how he would get into the building.

Officer Jerry Moore saw Susan sitting on the crate in her shop before she saw him. He slammed the patrol car door hard so he wouldn't frighten her. She turned and faced the entry as he walked through the door. "Good evening Ma'am," he drawled, "Miss Julia asked me to check on you for her. She just wanted to make sure you were okay. Okay?" Susan laughed, "Officer . . . ." "I'm sorry, ma'am. Officer Jerry Moore at your service. Don't tell Miss Julia I didn't give my name. She's kinda like my ma, and I don't want her feeling I'm not doing my job proper."

"It's our secret, Officer Moore," Susan replied. "And in regard to your question, I am okay and about to leave. It's been a long day and I need a good hot shower to clean off the dust."

"Well ma'am, if you're on your way home, I'll just sit out front until you lock up, if you don't mind. Miss Julia taught me Sunday School, and I make a point never to disappoint her," he explained very seriously.

You and everyone else in this town! Susan thought as she grabbed her purse and pulled out the key to the deadbolt. When the door was securely locked, she walked to her car and unlocked it. Before getting in, she turned and called goodnight to Officer Moore. He gave her a little salute. On the way home, she thought of Tony for the first time since coming to town. She felt good about her decision to leave West Palm Beach. She had known that she *had to leave,* but she had not really resolved in her mind until now the conflict she had felt in leaving. She didn't consider herself a quitter or a person to run away from trouble, but her decision had been the right one. She had pulled into the Martin driveway before she realized what had triggered her thoughts about West Palm Beach and Tony. Julia Martin was a very nurturing, and protective person. She had sent Officer Moore to make sure she was okay, not to keep a constant check on her movements. Tony had made her feel as though she was suffocating with his constant calls and unexpected appearances. One night, when a male client had walked her to her car, she recognized Tony's car parked on a side street. Remembering now, her stomach contracted with a spasm. That was the beginning of the end. She looked over and realized Jay was standing outside the front door. He bowed when he saw her look up and indicated the door. She got out and went up the walk. "Have I overlooked something?" she asked.

"Something very important," he said solemnly.

"I'm sorry," she said, flustered. He quickly countered, "Hey, hey, hey! No big deal. You're tired. You look beat. Come on in and I'll run you a hot bath and fix you a drink." Susan started laughing.

When she was inside the foyer, she stopped laughing and asked, "Will the real Jay Martin stand up?" His eyebrows went up in that quizzical manner, as he asked, "Which means?" Susan was just tired enough, and just slightly giddy enough to forge on as she said, "You're arrogant, abrasive, sweet, irritating, smart, thoughtful, gallant, and . . .". "Thirty-seven today," he said. "Today's your birthday?" she asked, incredulously. "All day," he quipped.

"Did Julia cook a special dinner tonight?" she asked. "Yes, she did," he answered. "Have you eaten?" she asked. "No, we haven't," he answered.

"Oh Jay, I am so sorry," she moaned.

"No problem, just do whatever you want to do. Take a bath. Don't take a bath. Eat if you want to, or don't eat if you don't want to. Have a drink, or don't have a drink, give me a birthday kiss, or don't give me a birthday kiss. No. I take that last one back."

"Which part of it?" she asked.

"I'll tell you later, after you've had a bath, drink, and food. Okay?" he asked.

"Very definitely okay," she said.

When Susan started for the kitchen, Jay stopped her. "Go get your bath. Julia is the kind of woman who runs on her own time and can handle a little delay. Besides, Henry is on another rampage—if you remember—for the second time this week. So Julia is next door."

Susan had decided to take Jay at his word and had her bath water running when she heard a knock on her bedroom door. She quickly slipped on her robe and opened the door. Jay was standing there with a tall exotic drink in his hand. There was even a small umbrella in it. "Room service," he said. "Thank you very much, Sir," she murmured, looking down in an exaggerated modest way. Jay cocked his eyebrow and lowering his voice, said, "Lovely lady, do not play coy with me, unless you want me to barge into your room, throw you on the bed, and . . . rub your back."

"Hey," Susan retorted, "I'll take you up on that." "Can't," Jay said, "Julia's back and says dinner will be ready in thirty minutes." "Oh, the bath!" Susan cried as she remembered the bath water and slammed the door in Jay's face. *Thank goodness the tub had not run over!*

The dinner was wonderful. Susan had studied for six months at a Cordon Bleu school in Paris, but Julia was a natural in the kitchen. After a hot bath, Jay's drink, and Julia's meal, her long day now seemed like a piece of cake. Susan asked about Henry and learned that the doctor had arranged for Velma to give Henry a shot when he got out of control. There was still a problem calming Henry down enough to give him a shot, so Julia had run to Velma's rescue.

Dinner over, Julia insisted that they leave the dishes for later and drink their desert wine out in the sunroom. The conversation was relaxed as Julia and Susan each recapped briefly the events of the day. Jay, the ever taciturn lawyer, quietly murmured an occasional, "uh huh," or similar syllable, indicating that he was listening. The heat of the afternoon sun coming through the large expanse of glass windows surrounding the room was absorbed by the Italian tiles on the floor, and even though the lateness of the evening was cool, the room was just warm enough to be comfortable. When Julia got up to leave, Susan stood up to follow her. "No, no, no," Julia protested. "You two stay out here and enjoy this beautiful spring evening. Susan, you've worked especially hard today, and Jay is the birthday boy." Susan sat back down on the small sofa, too mellowed-out to protest, and Jay, before Julia was out of the room, unabashedly came over, sitting down next to Susan, and slipping his arm around her back, rested it on the sofa. Although his arm was not touching her, she imagined she could feel its warmth, however, his firm leg slowly pressing against hers was not imagined. Remembering her earlier playful exchange with Jay, she became disturbingly excited with anticipation; so when he said, "Now, tell me again about Ralph Getz and his request about the key," for just a moment, Susan was disappointed. *What was I expecting him to do?*

Susan shook off the ambivalent feelings as she again related the exchange with Ralph. "Um." Jay said, as if reflecting on the account, then, "I hope you remembered the invitation to the dance on Saturday." *This man is like quicksilver,* she thought before replying, "I haven't really thought about it because you vaguely said this weekend, not a specific day, and as you know, my social calendar is crazy." Jay cocked his eyebrow at her in that maddening way, and said, "You know, you should have been a lawyer."

"You haven't tasted my cooking yet!" she retorted.

"Right now, there's only one thing I want to taste," he said, as he brought his arm around her shoulder, pulling her body against his. His kiss did not last long. It was just very thorough. Later, as Susan lay in her bed in the dark remembering, and yes, savoring that kiss, she analyzed it. *His lips were firm, no, soft and firm, and slightly open, and I felt just the slight tip of his tongue. God, he was tasting me!*

~7~

Pinkie took the last bite of his steak and washed it down with beer. He had limited himself to one mug. He needed to be cold sober when he went back to get in that building. While he didn't have a lot of respect for the law, it wouldn't be an easy task to get away from them in a place like Martinsville if they spotted him breaking and entering. As he drove back into town, he reflected on the other limitations of a job in a small place like this. No females were available. At least no females he could trust. One thing about a prostitute-she knew what she was. In a small town, the prostitutes weren't happy just being prostitutes. They wanted to tie some poor, dumb schmuck up in marriage, and then do the prostitute gig on the side—kind of a double dipping. At least a good professional prostitute gave you your money's worth and didn't give you any diseases or backtalk. He slowed down as he passed the city limits sign and drove to the spot where he had planned to park the car. Not spotting anyone, he parked and quickly got out and walked to the back of the building. The back door lock called for a specialist. Heavy-duty locks were not his specialty. Besides, there might be an alarm. He walked to the side of the building. It was hidden from the street, and no one was likely to come around at this time of the night. There was a utility pole with prongs for climbing next to the building, and an air-conditioning unit next to that. He climbed on top of the unit and then climbed the pole until he was parallel with the roof of the building. Even if he managed to jump to the roof, getting back down was impossible without breaking his neck. He climbed back down and took another look at the deadbolt on the back door. He'd have to find another way! Disgusted, he went back to his car and drove the couple of blocks to his motel. If he ever took on another job in a little burg like this, he'd be sure to bring a DVD player and some good porno flicks. For now he'd have to content himself with his bottle of Scotch and a late show on TV!

Officer Jerry Moore made up for his lack of shrewdness by going by the rules he had learned with high marks at the Police Academy. As he made his rounds tonight, he passed by the building where he had met Ms. Julia's friend, Susan, earlier. As he continued down the street, he noticed an unfamiliar car parked on a side street and was about to turn around and go back to check it out when the dispatcher came on the line giving him instructions to go out to the Smith dairy. The old man was drunk again and firing his rifle at the cows. *Poor Mrs. Smith.* Ever since the big dairy conglomerates had forced out the little dairy farmers like the Smiths, there were people like them that just couldn't cope. What was a person supposed to do when he was too old to learn a new trade, and everything he owned was tied up in that trade? As Jerry rode out to the Smith place, his thoughts were on the Smiths, and the strange car was completely forgotten.

On Friday morning Susan finished her run and half-expected to see Jay on her return to the house. She'd gone through a see-saw of emotions before starting her run and had almost talked herself out of going, then, mad at herself for acting like a foolish schoolgirl, she forced herself out the door. Now, she was disappointed because she'd rehearsed what she'd say when she met him, and he wasn't there! *I love being a female! So why in the hell is it so hard?* She could not imagine a man going through such convolutions of emotions. She had never felt more female in her life, but wasn't so sure it was worth having all these touchy, touchy feelings. This was not the sort of thing that a female discussed with her Dad, and it had been too long since her mother had died; she'd never had an opportunity to discuss it with her either.

Julia was as near to a mother as Susan had had in over fifteen years, but she certainly couldn't discuss it with her. Besides, the time for discussing *that* was too late. Julia was enjoying watching the dynamics between her son and Susan. But why? He had seemed like a boor at first, but he certainly was quite capable of snaring any available women. As she took her shower, she slowly turned off the hot water until she began to shiver from the cold. Feeling as though that was at least a stop-gap solution, she dried herself vigorously with a towel and dressed. She started to forgo breakfast, having lost her courage to face Jay this morning, then chided herself again and walked into the kitchen. Jay was over in the breakfast room with the newspaper opened before him. He looked up from his reading. "Well, it's about time!" he said.

"What do you mean by that?" she asked, confused that she might have misunderstood something that had been planned. Then continuing, "I've been up and ran as usual. Undoubtedly, you were not up to yours this morning,"

Jay quietly answered, "Lovely lady, I not only ran my usual two miles at the crack of dawn, I have been, what the poets call, walking on air. Do you suppose you could give me such inspiration every day?" Susan stood as though transfixed for a moment before she responded. She let out a laugh, part relief and part joy, walked over to where Jay was sitting and putting her arms around him, kissed him passionately on the mouth. He tasted deliciously like coffee and cinnamon. The kiss he returned was not the tasting kiss of the night before. This kiss was a hungry kiss; a kiss that explored her mouth in search of satiation.

When he finally let her go, Susan was so aroused, her face felt hot. "Perhaps," he said, "We can resume this again later. I hope you understand that you are not some casual flirtation that I am playing around with. Right now, however, I have a court date with a very demanding female judge who will not find exception to my being late to her court, especially if I have the peculiar look of Jack and his bean stalk. Okay?" Susan let go of Jay, saying, "Okay," and squelching a giggle—it was her turn to walk on air—she turned around and busied herself pouring a cup of coffee while Jay made a fast exit. When she heard his car back out of the driveway, she burst out loud with, "Yes, yes, yes!"

When Julia came in from tending her roses, Susan had calmed down, but was still feeling as if she needed, somehow, to purge the wild passion coursing through her body. Julia stopped, looked at her, and remarked, "You look positively radiant today. I wish I were young enough to run. By the way, tomorrow night won't be formal, and if you need anything, Madisons is your best bet." Susan was usually grateful for Julia's company. Today was an exception. She resigned herself to cleaning up the kitchen instead of taking another cold shower. Jay's words echoed in her mind, *you are not some casual flirtation that I am playing around with. No,* she thought, *and neither are you such to me.* With great reluctance Susan pushed romance from her mind and headed for work.

All day Susan tried to concentrate only on her work. She had planned the reception for Julia's friend, with canapés that could be prepared the day before. Julia's kitchen would be used to prepare the hot foods on the day of the reception. She had hired three people to help transport and serve the food. Until she trained a staff, all the food would be prepared only by herself. Susan's artistic bent was as much a part of her catering appeal as the taste of the foods that she prepared. For the food itself was visually a work of art and always included floral decorations as well as motifs requested by the client. Susan had never advertised her business in West Palm Beach. It just seemed to happen. Her reception and catering reputation brought in all the business she ever needed. But Susan had neither the reputation in Martinsville, nor was she familiar enough with the customs in the area to assume anything. Therefore, she needed to talk to both the client and the florist to make sure there were no misunderstandings. She had too much to do right now trying to get her shop ready, and now this catering job was pushing her. Ralph Getz's request that Susan safeguard the key to his side of the building had to be fulfilled if she wanted the electrical work done ASAP, so she struggled with arranging her activities around the electricians in order to enable them to finish; and as soon as they were finished with the main changes, the other workmen would be starting the partitions that would create different work areas.

Susan sensed, rather than heard someone behind her. She turned, expecting Jay to have slipped in to surprise her. Instead, a man of about thirty something was standing in the doorway. "Yes?" she asked, "May I help you?" His voice, when he answered, was as smooth and as rich as any MC that Susan had ever heard. His appearance was like a caricature and didn't match his voice. He wasn't quite what you would call ugly, just not appealing. He reminded her somewhat of the car dealer down in the little town where she had traded her Lincoln. "I was looking for a warehouse that someone told me about, but I must have the wrong location," he said. Susan replied, "I think you have the right location, but it's the other side of this building. Did Mr. Getz send you over?"

Pinkie was afraid a lie might be discovered and ruin his plans, so he answered, "No, I was talking to someone who suggested that the space was about what I need and just wanted to take a look before I spoke to the owner." Susan had enough to deal with concerning Ralph Getz and didn't want to play his real estate rep as well, so she just said, "The electricians are over there right now making some changes. It might be difficult for both you and them, if you go in right now. You could peek in the door to get some idea about the space, but otherwise I can't suggest anything except maybe calling and asking for an appointment.'

Pinkie was not going to be dissuaded, so he said, "The front door's locked." Susan's mind was saying *please go away*, but her voice said, "You'll have to go in the back door." Pinkie looked at the door in the back, and asked, "Can I use your back door?" Susan almost choked with exasperation, as she replied, "Yes, of course. follow me." She crossed the room to the door, turned the deadbolt, and started opening the door. Pinkie grabbed the edge of the door, pulled it halfway open, then stopped and examined the door. "Good lock. Good heavy door," he commented, "I want a place that's secure." Susan was beyond exasperated. She wanted to scream *yes, and I want you to go!* When he went out the back door, she slammed it as he was saying, "Thanks." What she *didn't* hear him saying under his breath, when the door slammed, was, "Damn Bitch!" And what she had no way of knowing was his looking at the door had given him the means for entry. Pinkie looked inside the door of the next unit. The workmen paid no attention to him at all as he ran his hand inside the door while watching them.

~8~

When Pinkie left the building, he had a very superior feeling. *Stupid hicks!* He had managed to spot the weakness in Susan's back door lock and had put a piece of metal in the opening of the lock next door. The lock on *her* door was a brand new deadbolt, apparently put in at her request. If he could gain access to both sides of the building, he could bring her to her knees in a week. Then he'd blow this dinky little burg. His thoughts reflected on the little brunette hooker in West Palm that usually took up his spare time. She was expensive, but she was worth it. He looked at his watch. Time for his siesta. The recently acquired habit of an afternoon nap might cause some trouble when he got back to West Palm. *Oh well, he thought, he'd have to figure that out when he got back home*. Probably after a week more of this, he'd be grateful to go back to his old routine, nap or not. Pulling up to his motel, he thought about trying that local hooker again, but nixing that, he went on into the motel room, took out his bottle of Scotch and turned on the TV. Today he was going to hear what Oprah had to say about men suffering from impotence. He ought to get a laugh out of this. What a crock. He thought again about the brunette in West Palm. Now *she* could cure any man's impotence, but he decided it wasn't a good idea to even think about her right now. With no brunette, and no porn, Pinkie decided to pour himself *four* fingers of Scotch. That would put him out of his misery for a few hours, and then . . .

While Pinkie drank himself into his afternoon state of oblivion in order to come out later like his kindred night creatures who do mischief under the veil of darkness; Susan, trapped in her innocent oblivion, was trying to lock the back door to Ralph Getz's place. It took three attempts before she finally got the door locked. All in all, it had been a productive, though harrowing day. The schedule had been finalized in regard to the reception she was catering next week. Frank Nigel had come by with the shop plans (that were perfect), and a contract (which she had gladly signed), and the electricians had finished the main changes; so now she could give Ralph Getz back his key *and suggest an appropriate place for him to put it!*

It was time to do something totally self-centered. She was going to take Julia's suggestion and run by Madison's before they closed. The thought of picking out something ravishing that would make her look less tired than she felt gave her a lift. But she had to hurry before they closed. Driving over to the shop, she admitted to herself she wanted to please Jay and Julia tomorrow night. *What is wrong with me? I'm acting like a foolish love-struck teeny bopper.* The parking places next to Madison's were taken so she had to drive around the block twice before a parking place opened up. She managed to get in the door five minutes before the store closed. The clerk was very pleasant under the circumstances and showed her the section where the dressier garments were.

Susan was flipping through the racks when the woman came over to her. Susan expected to hear, "I'm sorry, but we're closing now." Instead, the woman said, "I'm Margaret Madison, we haven't met, but I believe we have a mutual friend in Julia Martin." For a moment Susan wondered how Julia managed to keep all of the people in her life informed about what was taking place in her life and at the same time manage to do all of the other things she did. "Yes," she answered, "I'm Susan Sullivan, and right now I'm a guest in Julia's home. She's a wonderful lady." Margaret Madison excused herself, walked over to a closet behind a counter, and brought out three dresses, saying, "Would you care to look at these?" One was mauve, one was emerald green, and the last was an *iridescent* red. Susan checked the sizes. *My size.* "Did Julia pick these out?" she asked. Margaret just smiled and answered, "She described you, and suggested that you might be in today or tomorrow. I picked them out." "Thank you," was all Susan could think to say before asking, "And the dressing room?" "Right behind the large curtain," Margaret replied.

Susan quickly entered the large room behind the curtain. There were half a dozen small curtained stalls on either side of the room, with a mirrored wall at the back. She entered one of the stalls, stripped down to her underwear, and tried each dress on. When she had finished trying them all on, she was in a dilemma. She loved each one of them, and each one fit her as though it had been tailor-made just for her. When she stepped into the outer sales room, she imagined that Margaret Madison knew exactly what had taken place. "So, Susan—May I call you call you Susan?" she asked. "Of course," Susan replied. Margaret took the dresses from Susan, and said, "Please call me Margaret, Susan. Did you like any of the dresses?" "I'm afraid I like all of them," Susan said with a smile. "Then I'll put them on your account," Margaret stated, as though she had done business with her for years. Susan immediately protested, "Wait, wait, wait. I am trying to get my business started, and right now, as much as I would love to take every one of these dresses, I have to limit myself." "Tell you what, Susan. You take all three dresses and you'll have three months to pay for them, or return them. No strings attached. Okay?" Susan couldn't help but ask, "Do you think that's a good way to run a business?"

"As a matter of fact, I do," she replied, "You'll be running a catering service here in town. But, in a way, I run a catering service. I'm hoping that you do business with me in the future, instead of going over to Atlanta to shop." Susan laughed and said, "Not only can you pick out lovely dresses, you also have a straightforward way of doing business. So yes, I'll take all three. If I can't make it in three months, I'll never make it." With her purchases wrapped in garment bags, Susan thanked Margaret, and left.

It was six thirty when Susan pulled into the driveway at the Martin home. Julia's car was in the driveway, but there was no sign of Jay's. A little lemon of disappointment was quickly turned into a lemonade of relief. She would have Julia help her decide which dress she should wear tomorrow night. She took the garment bags out, went into the house, and located Julia. "Julia, I stopped at Madison's and picked out three dresses. I would appreciate your opinion in choosing a dress for tomorrow night." Julia was delighted to oblige. "You go slip into the first one while I check the stove," she said.

Susan decided on the red dress first. It was almost sinful looking on her. She then walked into the kitchen and caught Julia's attention. "Susan," Julia exclaimed, "You look absolutely gorgeous!" Susan was basking in the warmth of this woman's approval.

"Wait, Julia, before you give me an answer. Two more to go." When Susan returned, she had on the mauve dress. It was more demure with a high neck, but was made of a soft clinging chiffon that showed ever curve of her lovely shape. Again Julia let out a little exclamation of approval, "Susan, you are just too pretty for words!" When Susan walked back to her bedroom to try on the third dress, she remarked to herself, *I should be ashamed of myself, reveling in all this attention, but I love it!*

Susan's dad had never given her a moments doubt of his love, but there are just things that mothers understand about their daughters that dads don't. As she walked into the kitchen for the third time, there was a second right before she pirouetted when she knew that she and Julia were not alone. After full circle, she stopped, and there stood Jay. He cocked *that eyebrow*, and whistled before saying," I think you are going to have to toss a coin. You look beautiful in every one of them." "No, Susan," Julia disagreed, "I don't think you should toss a coin. Which one would you like to wear tomorrow night?"

Jay walked over to the wine cabinet, pulled out a bottle of the pinot blanc, and started opening it as he said under his breath, "Females, females, why do I love females so much?" As both Susan's and Julia's head turned to face him, he asked, "What? Why are you both looking at me like that?" Susan turned back to face Julia, and asked, Which one do you think I should wear tomorrow night?" Julia said emphatically, "Dear, you look wonderful in each of them." Susan had been around Julia long enough to know how her mind worked. "So, what did you have in mind?"

Julia was not a woman who was afraid of giving her opinion. "The mauve is perfect for a wedding, so you might want to keep that in reserve. The red is perfect for the July fourth dance at the club, and that's only two months away. That leaves the green. You are absolutely stunning in it." "Thanks, and I agree," Susan concurred, then realizing what she had meant, versus what she had said, tried to explain. "Susan," Julia stopped her, "I know what you *meant.* Go take your lovely dress off, and then we'll have dinner." Jay smiled as *that* picture was conjured up in his mind. Susan had also learned how Jay's mind worked by now and so quickly retreated before he saw she was blushing.

~9~

When Susan returned, the table was set, and Julia served dinner. "I wish you'd waited and let me at least set the table Julia," she said, "I don't know how you do all your activities without domestic help." Julia responded with a smile and explained. "Jay set the table for me, and I have a marvelous woman who is now in Alabama attending her ailing mother. It's sad to say, but she will probably remain there until she buries the good woman. I can do without Willa Mae for as long as it takes her to do what she has to do." Susan looked at Jay who responded by saying, "Susan, I'm sure you learned to do a few things that are associated with the male gender. I don't think it hurts my masculinity to set the table. Did you think I was just a handsome face?" Susan wondered how Jay was able to bounce back and forth between the astute lawyer and the clown and still have people take him seriously. Then she laughed. Probably because he was good at both!

The dinner was superb, as usual, but the talk was bordering on restrained. Susan wondered if the mention of Julia's employee's mother dying brought back some sad memories for Julia that had been buried under the busyness of public service. And Jay's loss? Susan now knew that the man who talked his way through a court room, also talked his way through rooms in his mind that he dared not open to others. She couldn't believe that it had been less than a week ago that she had asked herself who Jay was? That question had gone from a simple identification question, to a rhetorical question, and finally to a deeper philosophical question. She felt peaceful now, feeling that she knew the answer. If someone had asked her if she thought it possible to fall totally, and inexplicably in love in the course of five days, she would have considered that person mentally unstable. What would her father say, if he were still alive? *Go for it, honey!* If only her dad had lived long enough to meet the Martins.

Susan was suddenly aware that Julia and Jay were looking at her and waiting for an answer. "I'm sorry," she apologized, "I'm afraid I was thinking about . . . . something, . . . else." Julia spoke, "I said I wonder if I did you a disservice by referring Mildred Brice to you at this time. You seem more tired than usual this evening." Susan protested, "No, no, not at all. Everything is planned, and scheduled. I have an appointment with the florist, and also Mildred on Monday. I had a couple of unexpected interruptions today that had nothing to do with the business, but those things happen. I shouldn't be in business if I can't handle the unexpected. And I want you to let me clean up the kitchen or I'll be terribly upset." Julia knew when she had to give in. She and Susan had a lot in common. "Sounds great to me, I'm somewhat tired tonight. In fact, if you kids don't mind, I'm going to retire to my bedroom." When Julia left, Jay stood up, saying, "I'll help," then started gathering dishes, and silverware, and carried them to the kitchen. He and Susan worked together, neither talking, until the kitchen was clean and the dishes, pots, and pans were put away. Susan had grown accustomed to Jay's banter, and now wanted desperately for him to break the silence that had invaded their space. When the last dish was put away and the last towel hung up, Jay reached out and pulled Susan to him. "You're not afraid of anything, are you?" "Not now," she replied. His kiss that followed was not a passionate kiss, but brief as though he were putting a seal on an unspoken covenant between the two. Continuing to hold her, he ran his hands gently over her back before hugging her securely to him, then released her, saying, "Lovely lady, sleep well. I'll see you in the morning." As he stepped back, he reached out and traced the outline of her lips with his finger before turning and walking to his room.

Jay closed the door to his bedroom, walked over to where the picture albums were kept in the bottom of a book case, and selected an album. Then he walked over to a small chaise and sat down, flipping through the pages of the album. Somehow, the visual images grounded him. He located the picture of himself with his father. Jay looked like the young conquering hero in his Air Force uniform, while his father's appearance sharply contrasted to Jay's, emphasizing the older man's dire condition. Jay still remembered the afternoon this particular photo was taken and the choice he was forced to make that day still brought him pain. He thought now about that choice as he had so many times since then and wondered if he had known at that time that he would never see his father alive again, would his decision have been the same? Probably. The old man, as Jay affectionately called him, would not have made any other choice possible. There was a credo handed down in the family: "When your country needs you, you go." But what if your father is dying?. Jay sat and wondered, *why am I drinking from this bitter cup again?* Then his mind went to Susan and the telephone call related to her *real* reason for being in Martinsville. The DA had called him into his office this afternoon and told him that the FBI had called about Susan. They had traced her whereabouts to Martinsville and wanted to talk to her about some mob connection in West Palm Beach.

The information had jolted Jay. He could not imagine anyone like Susan having a mob connection. He thought about all the cases he had handled through the years. You don't practice law without developing some acumen and the his ability to judge people's character scored high in that regard.

As a lawyer, he approached people front and center. In fact, he'd started out with Susan in the same manner, but now? *I love this woman!* Remembering Susan modeling her new dresses for Julia, unaware he was watching, convinced him further of her innocence. This is a smart, independent, and hard working woman, but he was also aware of an almost adolescent innocence she worked hard to conceal. She was certainly not some gun moll! He got up and crossed to his door. Opening it, he went down the hall, and knocked on Susan's door. When she opened the door, she had a puzzled look on her face. "Yes, Jay?"

"We need to talk," he said in a low voice. "Where?" she asked. "It doesn't matter to me," he said. "Wherever you're comfortable." "Come in," she said and stepped away from the door. She pointed to the chair next to her bed and sat on the edge of the bed. "What's this about?" Susan's look of confused expectancy distressed Jay. He knew no other way to ease her discomfiture except to quickly come to the point. "The DA called me in today. It seems the FBI contacted his office in order to find out information about you in regard to the Vascola family operation down in West Palm Beach." A muted cry escaped Susan's mouth that sounded like a wounded animal. Jay continued, "I don't pretend to assume anything about what has happened in your past, but if you need a lawyer, I can't represent you. I'm in love with you. It would not be to either of our best interests for me to do so. However, if you need money, that's not a problem, and I can get you the best lawyer in the state."

Susan wanted to get up and leave. The humiliation was too much. But instead, she tried Jay's acerbic tactic and said,. "I thought you were the best in the state." Jay was totally disarmed. His voice sounded hurt as he softly answered, "No, not really."

When Susan begin to weep, Jay moved to the bed next to her and cradled her in his arms. "Don't cry, please don't cry. I may not know what this is all about, but I know you didn't do anything that merits the FBI coming after you." Jay felt a little shudder go through Susan, then she regained control, although her voice now came out in almost a whisper, "I was afraid of *him*, and I was afraid of the FBI. I had to get away. I don't know anything about the Vascolas except that they're despicable people. I made the mistake of dating Tony, and then he started stalking me. At first I couldn't believe it. He denied it, of course. But I saw him. Finally, when a rumor started circulating that the Vascolas were under investigation, I had to get away. I knew nothing about their affairs. I didn't *want to know* anything about their affairs, but I knew if I stuck around, my name would be connected to theirs in everyone's mind and my business would go down hill. I did nothing wrong. I did . . . . nothing wrong." By the time Susan had finished her explanation, she was sobbing and Jay was gently rocking her in his arms. "Susan, Susan, everything is going to be fine." His comforting kiss on the cheek became a catalyst drawing their lips together and the passion of yesterday became kindled again. "God, woman, you are killing me," he murmured, restraining himself. "I hate to take cold showers at this time of the night!" Susan made a decision. He had had her in a position where she was vulnerable and made the choice not to exploit her. He was everything good she had concluded him to be. "Please don't take a cold shower," she said as she loosened her robe. Jay stood up, removing his clothes and Susan's robe, as she turned back the covers on the bed.

~10~

Pinkie awoke with a hangover. It was hard to believe that one more finger of Scotch would bring on a hangover. He looked at his watch—eight thirty. Still too early to go to the warehouse. He decided some food might help his stomach, so he got up, splashed water over his face, and combed his hair. Twenty minutes later, he was almost to the little eating joint near the interstate. By ten, he had eaten, and was back on the road again heading back to Martinsville. He was not sure that Friday night was a good time to be doing what he had planned. Teenagers were usually out roaming around on Friday night. The only thing that prompted him to stick with his plan was knowing the shop was not in an area frequented by kids. He decided to leave his car, a familiar sight at the motel, and walk to the building. He had taken off the rental tag and put on another one, but a strange car could be spotted in a town this size. Once he reached the area, it took only a little effort to jimmy the lock to the door on the vacant side of the building, open it, and slip in. He closed the door, hoping there would be access into Susan's place from the interior of the building. There was a street light shining in from a high window. He switched on a small penlight and cast the beam on the floor as he explored the large inside space. *Damn!* There was no inside door connecting the two sides of the building. However, Pinkie discovered there was a smaller room within the large space, an office probably. Pinkie was curious as to why the owner chose to keep an old flimsy lock on the outside door, while securing an inside door with a deadbolt. He shined the light on the deadbolt and studied it to see if he could get it open. He pulled out a bunch of keys from his jacket pocket and felt for the small stop on the ring that was the beginning of the series of keys. Methodically he tried each key, one by one, until he found one that almost fit. He tried the next key, a little better. Finally, after exerting a little twist on the key, the deadbolt turned and he opened the door.

His penlight revealed a room about twelve by twelve with no windows. He closed the door and turned on an overhead light. *Sweet!* Against one wall there were file cabinets and a desk with a computer on it, while unfamiliar machinery was taking up a lot of the other space. Pinkie had operated on the wrong side of the law long enough to spot an illegal operation, and he was looking at one now. But what? He avoided the computer. He had never had any desire or reason to use a computer, and he had an uncertainty about them that bordered on fear. He opened one of the file cabinets and started to peruse the files. Nothing there to arouse suspicion. Closing the file drawer, he turned to the equipment, looking at each different piece of equipment, trying to imagine how it was related, and then it hit him. Someone was making counterfeit cards of some kind! He tried to read the metal type, couldn't, thought about the files, but decided that he needed to stick to his plan. Maybe his boss could use this operation in the future. Right now he had to concentrate on the woman. With this in mind, he looked around to make sure he hadn't disturbed anything that would give this Ralph whatever a reason to be suspicious. Satisfied, he walked to the door, switched off the light and opened the door. The light from the street lamp gave him the confidence to step out and turn back to lock the door. He never knew what hit him. The man who had hunted and killed his prey so efficiently in the past was now the prey—a dead one. The tire wrench had crushed the back of his skull.

Ralph Getz stepped over the body and opened the door to the room the victim had just left. Ralph pulled the body into the room, closed the door and switched on the light. He rolled the body over and looked at the man's face. *Who in the hell is this?* Ralph did not recognize the man. Was that good or bad? If the man had just stumbled into the place to burglarize it, that wouldn't be so bad. Ralph could just call the law. But why would anyone go to the trouble to burglarize an obscure warehouse? Suppose someone got wind of what he had been doing? No. That was impossible unless . . . unless the authorities were on to him. Ralph was clearly rattled. He had to get a handle on himself.

He went over to the desk, pulled out the bottom drawer, lifted out a fifth of bourbon and a glass, poured himself a stiff drink, and downed it in one continuous swallow. He couldn't take a chance. He sat down at the chair behind the desk and formulated a plan. He knew where he could get rid of the body, but how about the unknowns? Was the man working alone? Where was he staying? Ralph had to know the answers to these questions before he could act. No sense in painting himself into a corner. His life was at stake. He went over to the man and went through his pockets. There was a rental car key and a motel key in one pocket and a set of burglar's keys in the other. Then he checked his back pockets. A handkerchief in one and a billfold in the other. Ralph opened the billfold and looked at a Florida driver's license with a picture of one Adolph Rieser. Ralph took a second look at the dead man's face and confirmed his identity. Suddenly Ralph became aware of the possibility that he was leaving finger prints on the everything. Once again, Ralph had to pull himself together. He grabbed an old towel he kept in the room and wrapped it around the man's head to keep it from bleeding all over the place. He checked his watch. Ten minutes after eleven. He knew Jerry Moore's routine. He had exactly ten minutes to get the body into the trunk of his car before Jerry made his round. He pulled the man over to the outside door and left him while he opened his car trunk.

He was sweating by the time he had gotten the body into the trunk and locked it. He went back inside long enough to sweep up some sawdust the electricians had left and dumped it on the floor where the man had bled. *That'll have to do until tomorrow!* He went back out and got into his car and was down the street on his way in record time to the motel where *Adolph* was staying. He only hoped that all the scum that occupied that rat's nest were either drunk, or engaged with the town hooker. When he got to the motel, he took the key and opened the door. He let out a breath of relief as he surveyed the empty room. No confederate and no hooker! He grabbed the man's bag in the floor of the closet and quickly went through the entire room, pulling out all the drawers and looking under the bed for anything that might identify him, then stuffed everything into the bag. It took Ralph all of ten minutes to clear the motel room. He wiped everything he touched, including the doorknob and key, which he left in the outside of the lock. He hoped someone *would* spot the key and make themselves at home in a free room. That would help cover any potentially incriminating tracks he may have left behind. He went over to the car parked in front of the room he had just left, and pulling the strange key out, tried it in the lock. Bingo! He quickly walked around the car and looked at the license tag. "Umm." Bogus!

Back in his car again, he drove out to his farm and cut across the field. He drove up to the remains of the old farmstead his parents had reared him in and stopped. Less than fifteen minutes later, he had the body of Adolph and his belongings peacefully resting at the bottom of the old well. He couldn't help but chuckle to himself. He had already asked Bart Dilbert to fill the old well in last week. Bart told him he would do it in about a week. Meanwhile, if he didn't show up by a day or two, Ralph would dump in the two bags of lime left over from his spring planting. He couldn't embalm the fellow, but he might keep him from stinking.

Ralph got back into his car and used his cell phone to call his contact up in Tennessee, asking him to send a wrecker *immediately* to the Day's Rest in Martinsville to tow the rental car to Atlanta to the rental agency where he was to leave the car anonymously. He mentioned that there was a bogus tag on the car that had to be removed and replaced with the one under the driver's seat. By midnight, Ralph Getz was in his bed, snoring. If his wife ever wondered about Ralph's affairs, she had enough sense to keep it to herself after questions earlier in the marriage had been answered with Ralph's backhand. Meanwhile, Ralph slept as though he was the smartest man on the face of the earth. However, he didn't know it, but he had been extremely lucky instead of smart. Three minutes after Ralph pulled out from behind his building in town, Jerry Moore made his round, and this time he had actually driven around behind the building. When Jerry left, after checking the building, he drove past the motel where he again missed Ralph by three minutes. Blind luck.

~11~

Jay had reluctantly left Susan's bed in the wee morning hours. If he had thought it would not cause problems for Susan in the future, he would have asked her to marry him today. He knew someone who would be willing to issue a marriage license, he knew someone who would perform the ceremony, and he knew his mother would be delighted!

He also knew that his earlier judgment about Susan was correct—she was no gun moll! In fact, he knew now that she was even more innocent than he thought possible in this day and time, especially for a woman of thirty-two. Susan had never made love to a man before. Jay knew as he dressed for his golf game that *that* fact was irrefutable. He was so much in love with her that it was not something he had even given any thought to. But last night in the throes of run away passion, he discovered the truth. The hot shower had felt unusually good this morning, soothing his body parts. He knew Susan would be late getting up, and perhaps even a little shy after last night. He was determined to play his usual eighteen holes of golf today and give her an opportunity to be alone with her thoughts. There was something else he wanted to do. Dear Julia. Julia had taken Susan in knowing what he now knew—Susan was incredible. Jay had always known his mother to be a woman above other women, and that was probably the reason he had chosen not to marry. He wanted, as the song says, *a girl like the girl that married Dear ole Dad.* Julia, whether psychic or sage, had somehow recognized the qualities that Jay wanted in a wife were to be found in Susan, and steered her into his life. *Yes, Susan is quite a woman. Just like my mother!*

When Jay walked into the kitchen, Julia was sitting at the breakfast table reading the newspaper. Before Jay poured his coffee, he leaned over and kissed Julia on the cheek. "Good morning," he said, "Mind doing me a favor?"

"And good morning to you," she answered, "And yes. What do you need.?" His voice sounded very matter of fact, as he said, "Call Valerie at the florist and have a dozen red roses delivered to Susan. The card should read: I love you. Will you marry me?" Julia was totally noncommittal when she asked, "Do you want the card to have your name printed on it?" Jay had poured his coffee and sat down by now. "No, he replied," If she doesn't know who it's from, I'm in trouble." Julia looked up from her paper. "Congratulations, Dear. I think Susan will make a fine wife." Jay almost laughed at Julia's quiet pose of innocent noninvolvement but judiciously kept silent. *Yes, you conniving old hussy, you did a great job!* Jay reached over and slipped the financial page out of the paper and drank his coffee while scanning the financial news. Ten minutes later he stood up, said, "Thank you, Dear Julia. See you later," and left.

Susan was still in bed sleeping, but not so peacefully. She dreamed she was driving down the road with her Dad, and after a while the person beside her was not her Dad, it was Tony Vascola. She tried to stop him, but he kept reaching out and touching her. Finally, crying and fighting to keep the careening car on the road, she turned to tell him to leave her alone, and Jay had taken his place. Susan abruptly awakened. The dream was still vivid in her mind, and she realized that she had actually been crying as she wiped the tears with the edge of the sheet. Remembering the frantic passion of their lovemaking, she suddenly felt shy and slightly embarrassed. How can anything that wonderful be wrong? She was teetering on an emotional see saw. *He would have respected my decision. I pushed him.* Susan was determined not to feel guilty. She was not a young school girl, and Jay was certainly not an immature youth. They were both aware of the responsibilities of an adult relationship.

Slowly getting out of bed, Susan winced as she walked to the bathroom and turned on her shower. *Oh for the wonderful curative powers of hot water!* She would take a quick shower and then do her run. Fifteen minutes later she started out of the house just as a florist van pulled into the driveway. The young man passed her with a nod and started up the walkway as she ran down the sidewalk. Thirty minutes later Susan was back and exhausted, not so much from the run, but from the thoughts that were nagging away at her mind. When she went into the kitchen, there, propped next to the coffee maker, was a note from Julia. It read, "Dear Sleeping Beauty, I have measured out the coffee and water. Just turn on and enjoy. Love, Julia P.S. There is French toast left over in the fridge. Also took the liberty of going into your room and leaving a delivery that came for you. See you later." Susan glanced at the note, wondering what *that* was about, then turned on the coffee maker, took the French toast out of the fridge and popped it into the microwave, hitting the one minute time spot as she left the kitchen going to her room. *The florist*! When she opened her bedroom door, there on the small table by the window sat a dozen red roses. She walked over and removed the card and opened it. She read it, then read it again. After that she fell across the bed giggling like a giddy school girl. Then she cried until all the pent up emotions were exhausted, got up and went back to the kitchen where she sat down, calmly ate her breakfast, and thought: *Yes, yes, yes!*

The euphoria from the proposal was not long-lasting. By the time Susan had finished breakfast, she realized the significance of the DA's talk with Jay. Would or could this sort of thing bring any type of scandal to the Martin name? Susan had some serious thinking to do. She had gotten up from the table and was cleaning up her dishes when Julia came in. Susan couldn't allow Jay's love for her to jeopardize the Martin's position in the community. Susan had never been a person to avoid a necessary duty.

"Good morning," Julia said, while Susan stood trying to think *how* to say what she wanted to say. "Good morning, Julia. I need to talk to you about something." *That was a start!* "Of course, Dear," Julia replied. "Julia, when I came here I was running away from something. I have done nothing wrong, but I dated a man who ended up stalking me. I had other reasons to leave also. But anyway, Jay has asked me to marry him and I couldn't possibly marry him if you felt that I had intentionally deceived you or would do anything that would bring scandal to your family." The words had rushed out, and Susan stood breathlessly awaiting Julia's response. Julia walked over to Susan and gently said, "Susan, I hope you don't think I'm a prying old woman, but I knew everything about you by the end of the first day. You sat at my breakfast table and told me enough to have your references checked, and you passed with flying colors. If a family hasn't earned people's confidence enough to weather a little scandal, they need to shore up their reputation." Susan was dumbfounded but before she could say anything, Julia continued, "I would like for you to come on out to the sun room and meet your new family-to-be, okay?" Susan simply nodded her head in compliance and followed her.

Julia and Susan spent the next two hours going through the photo gallery of six generations of Martins and Prescotts. There were a few side excursions as Susan's curiosity was piqued by other photos. They were getting ready to end the session when Jay came in at two o'clock. He walked into the sun room and went directly to Susan where he leaned down and kissed her. "May I have my answer now?" he asked. Before Susan could answer, Julia stood up, gathered her arms full of the photo albums, and announced, "I believe it's time for a little lunch. You kids excuse me while I go prepare a chef's salad. Jay, did you eat at the club?" Jay, sitting down and taking Susan's hands in his, answered, "Sounds good to me." Julia smiled to herself as she left the room. *Reminds me of his father the day he proposed to me.*

Thirty minutes later Julia appeared and told Susan and Jay lunch was ready in the breakfast room. The couple were obviously not interested in food at the moment; however, Julia was the one person capable of completely rational thinking at the moment, so coaxed them into lunch, talking about the salad she had made *just for them*, and choosing words that had slight overtones of martyrdom. Realizing that Julia was completely out of character, Jay and Susan got up and went to the breakfast room. Julia was already seated and looking very . . . . *what?* Jay couldn't quite put his finger on this mood. Susan was too happy to sense anything except Jay, who seated Susan and after sitting down, asked. "All right Julia, what's up? Julia smiled and commented, "Jay, you are so much like my Dad, I am amazed—I get nothing past you!"

"All right, Julia, I know how much you revered Granddad, so I'm flattered, but you still haven't answered my question," Jay pressed.

Julia sat for a moment, as if collecting her thoughts. "Susan, Jay and I have been engaged in a parent/child dance for all his life. Sometimes I lead, and sometimes he does. I guess the thing that has kept our relationship healthy has been mutual respect. So keep this in mind before you make any decision. First, I'm so very pleased that Jay has proposed to you. I knew it was coming: I just didn't realize how soon. But, now I have a proposal of my own. Jay, you remember my friend in Atlanta, Dotty Nesmith. I called her on Friday." Julia turned to Susan to explain, "Dotty was my roommate at Agnes Scott College. She and I have maintained our friendship over the years, and her son is now the director of the local office of the FBI in Atlanta. I have taken it upon myself to call Dotty and explained your dilemma and asked her to talk to her son. He has agreed to take a deposition from you, hopefully in lieu of your returning to West Palm Beach. And Jay, I think Susan would probably welcome your moral support as well as your legal expertise. Okay, now both of you have a perfect right to call me an interfering old woman and tell me to mind my own business." Susan had never seen a less than totally confident Julia Martin until this moment, but Jay spoke up before Susan could say anything. "Julia, you're an interfering old woman that I love as much as life itself. Sometimes when I feel like asking you to mind your own business, I find your wisdom prevails." For a moment, Susan felt as if someone had knocked the breath out of her but before she could intercede on Julia's behalf, Jay continued, "However, since we are in the same mind frame, I'll forgive you as usual. I called Bruce Nesmith yesterday, and he agreed to the deposition. We both laughed when he told me you had already called Dotty."

Julia, recalling from whom this scion had descended and feeling secure in the affection she and her son shared, was totally unruffled by Jay's revelation, so turned to Susan and asked, "Susan, are you sure you can tolerate our bold and presumptuous natures?" Susan, who had finally caught up with the true meaning of the mother and son's exchange, remarked, "I'm starting to understand—difficult though it is—just give me time. I'm usually a fast learner."

"How about the trip to Atlanta?" Julia queried. Jay and Susan looked at one another before he answered, "We could make it a multipurpose trip." His provocative suggestion caused the color to rise in Susan's face, again leaving her with a sense of confusion. *Multipurpose trip?* Susan felt as though she were caught up in an out of body experience! But with *this* man, surrender was inevitable, so she slowly nodded.

~ 12 ~

After plans were made for the trip to Atlanta on Monday, Susan went to her room to try to sort out her feelings, look at where she was, both mentally and physically, and solitarily decide if that was where she truly wanted to be. She felt as if she had been shot out of a cannon and landed in cotton. In less than a month she had gone from a totally unacceptable position into a fairy tale. No one had twisted her arm, pressured her into making any of the decisions that she had made. *That's what was driving her crazy right now!* This was not like the serpent in the Garden of Eden, nor The devil proposing a deal with Daniel Webster. Susan knew in a visceral way that Julia and Jay were exactly what they seemed to be—good, honest, and caring people. No, they were a head and shoulders above anyone else. That's where her problem was. *Can I trust myself to make a decision that is going to have such far-ranging consequences?* When this question confronted her, Susan realized for the first time how much she had devalued herself by associating with the Lascolas! That she even questioned whether she was worthy of the best, showed just how much the events of the previous six months had eroded her sense of self worth. She felt a sadness for just a moment before the Sullivan spirit kicked in. Susan recognized the difference between the Lascola's pressuring tactics and the Martin's helpful nurturing style. Yes, things had escalated with Jay, but she knew the relationship was one of kindred souls. Remembering her doubts that constantly surfaced when dealing with the Lascolas, Susan was sure that what she now had with the Martin's was good, and after going over everything satisfactorily in her mind, she lay down for a nap.

At five o'clock, Susan was awakened by knocking on her door. It was Jay. "May I come in, beautiful lady?" he asked. *There was that eyebrow up again!* Breathlessly, Susan lifted her head and looked across the wadded sheet under her chin and answered, "I'm not sure you should come in. The last time was a little volatile." Jay smiled as he walked across to the bed, reached down and pulled a curl that had fallen across Susan's face, then said very softly, "I talked to Maurice a few minutes ago. He's given me the name of a diamond wholesaler in Atlanta. And until that diamond is placed on your finger, I've told myself I can wait." Susan looked steadily at Jay, and murmured, "Now you have to tell me." Jay wasn't sure he should even be in Susan's room. He cocked his head to one side and said, "Whoa! In that case, I *know* I'd better leave." Susan lifted her covers, swung her legs to the floor and stood up next to Jay. He took her in his arms and kissed her long and hard, feeling her body tremble, then said, "Dear lady, we might even have to make kisses off-limits." His hot breath warmed her cheek, as he held her tightly against him. "Jay, I feel foolish asking you," Susan remarked, "But are you sure?"

"Sure?" Jay asked with emotion. "Woman, are you aware that I have never behaved like this over a female in my entire life? Are you aware that I have dreams about you that even make me blush? Are you aware that I dare not even think about you in public for fear of certain anatomical parts rearing up and embarrassing me and the people around me? Can imagine what people would say. 'Jay, what are you up to, or, are you just up? But, enough of this erotic schoolboy confession. I want to spend the rest of my life with you. I want you to have my children. Okay?"

"Yes, Jay," Susan answered. "So," Jay said, feeling drained as though he had just tried a case in court, "We need to leave for the club in an hour. I'll see you then. Okay?" "Yes, Jay," Susan said again, then turning, walked over and opened her door. Jay made his exit. Before closing the door she said, "I love you too."

An hour later, Susan walked out into the foyer and turned to look for Julia and Jay. She heard Julia's voice before she saw her sitting in the afternoon shadows of the unlighted living room. "Susan! You look absolutely stunning!" Jay, sitting opposite Julia, stood up, walked over, and just stood there looking at her. The lights from the chandelier in the foyer shone on Susan's red hair, giving it the appearance of spun gold. The emerald green silk dress fitted her perfectly, revealing every exquisite curve of her body. Jay finally spoke, "I'm of two minds: I want to show you off, but I'm almost selfish enough not to want to share you with anyone. Julia is right; you are absolutely beautiful." Susan wanted to protest, but she knew to do so would have prolonged her discomfiture, so she smiled and asked, "Thank you, did I hold you up?" Julia turned and bent over the table where she had sat a bottle of wine and asked, "Susan, Jay, Would you mind? I would like to propose a toast to the prospective bride and groom. We can delay going to the club for a few minutes. You kids will have to forgive me, I'm not a young woman and I have visions of sugarplums dancing through my head. Not the kind you eat, however; I'm thinking of the two-legged kind." She handed Susan and Jay their wine and added, "You know, little Susan and little Jay?"

Jay laughed and said, "Susan, you can see how shameless this woman is. If she had her way, we'd be living in sin before the wedding." Jay bent over and kissed Julia on the cheek and murmured, "I love you dear, but patience please. We don't want Susan thinking I'm marrying her as a baby factory!"

"Okay," Julia countered, I'll be good. Now let me propose a toast handed down in our family. Beaming with a sanguine look of gratification at the part that she had played in this *coup du ciel*, Julia raised her glass as she quoted to Susan and Jay, "*May God rain his love and goodness down on you; may he bless your union with children and a bounty of material things that will satisfy all your needs, and may you always love and respect one another as much as you do now. Salute!*"

The evening spent at the Martinsville Country Club was both wonderful and excruciatingly uncomfortable at times. Susan's appearance in the green dress was enough to merit more attention than she was comfortable with, but being with the Martins magnified that attention. The green of Susans's dress seemed to be reflected in the faces of some of Jay's former women-friends. And to add to the chagrin of these women, the admiring glances from the men only served to fuel their envy. At sixteen, Susan would have innocently basked in the sensation she now generated, but at thirty-two, she was acutely aware that she was possibly alienating women she would like to count among her friends in the future. Finally though, Susan abandoned her sense of reticence, resolved herself to mending fences and placating adversaries later, when, after eating, Jay took her out on the dance floor. For a man of less than a nimble appearance, Jay was an outstanding dancer.

He danced a waltz with grace; he danced a jitter-bug with vigor; he danced a rumba with a sensual tease that embarrassed Susan.

When a tango was introduced by the band, Susan was ready to sit down; however, Jay continued to hold her hand and was not moving. The entire dance floor was abandoned by everyone except the two of them. Jay pulled her to his chest and started the dance. Due to her many years in dance training, Susan had performed many times in dance recitals from early youth to budding womanhood. But never had she experienced fear of a mistake until now. As Jay led her around the dance floor, she thought of this dance as a foreshadowing of her future with this enigmatic man who was: exacting to the point of abrasiveness, passionate in pursuit of his interests, and yet tender and protective of love ones and honor. By the end of the dance, she was satisfied that his step was so sure and his strength so great, that she could follow him wherever he led her, dance floor or otherwise. When the dance ended, Jay spun her out and took a bow as the appreciative applause resounded in the room.

The room buzzed with talk as they seated themselves. Jay reached over and took Susan's hand; as he pressed it to his lips, he looked into her eyes, and asked, "Will you forgive me? At times I can be a bit of an exhibitionist." Susan turned Jay's hand over and kissed it in return, then said, "Anytime you can do anything as well as you just did, I'll approve. I won't bother to ask how you happened to learn to dance like that. *Julia!*" "Dear lady," Jay answered, "I am caught between the wiles of two remarkable women. I am putty in your hands."

Later when the Martins left the club with Susan, those remaining stayed to *discuss* the newcomer until the lights were dimmed as an indication of closing time. Needless to say, the only criticism that could be attributed to Susan was the fact that she was a stranger in town. Her conduct was that of a lady. Her beauty had graced the club, and, unfortunately, created resentment among Jay's former *inamorata.*, and fear among the wives whose husbands were a little too outspoken in their admiration. But everyone's unspoken regard for the Martins was such that each person that had been a participant in the late—hour discussion knew that he or she must never say anything that would cast any dispersions on the Martins whose impeccable reputation could stand them against the best. Whatever future Susan had with them was for them and her to decide.

Meanwhile, seemingly oblivious to the furor that Susan's appearance had wrought, Julia went to bed happy, and true to his word, Jay kissed Susan goodnight at her door.

~ 13 ~

Tony Vascola was not a man to be thwarted by anyone; even a woman like Susan Sullivan was not to be excepted, but neither was a substandard ghoul like Pinkie whose talents were, at best limited and at worst, expendable. Tony had heard nothing from Pinkie since he had called after arriving in Martinsville, and that had been three days ago. Tony had called the cell phone assigned to Pinkie without any response. No answer. No voice mail. Nothing! Tony was now under the watchful eye of the local covey of FBI agents in the area and couldn't afford to send anyone else local to check on what was going on up in Georgia. He had brooded over the possibility that if the FBI located Susan, she *might* have some bit of information that might be of use to them, but he was sure she knew nothing of importance about the Vascola's operations in the area. What she had unknowingly taken with her, Tony had to have back, but what he craved more than anything was to bring Susan to her knees. No woman had ever bested him. Never! But with the FBI dogging his every move, he was limited in handling the situation from this far away. The beautiful bitch had just about given her business away, paid off all her staff, and covered her tracks *except for internet.* When Susan hadn't answered his calls by Monday morning, he had gone over to her shop and then her home. She had taken only her most treasured possessions and a few clothes. The love he had felt for her was gone and only a searing hurt which he nursed with a relentless desire for revenge was filling that terrible void in his very heart and soul. Of all the hurts that a human can sustain, nothing can turn from so lofty a passion to so bitter a vendetta as the hurt of an egoist whose love has been rejected. Police reports are full of written accounts of the aftermath of such hurts. He didn't want Susan dead, he wanted her brought down alive—to suffer.

Tony finally got through to a fellow Mafioso in New Orleans on his cell phone and had a *chat.* He said nothing incriminating and yet the language defied only those *not* of the Brotherhood. When the call ended, the only thing left to finish the plan was a message by special courier delivered to a local inactive relative. In the twenty-first century, unsevered ties go back for hundreds of years.

Tony had been limited to how much pressure he could exert on Susan's defunct staff. They were loyal beyond reason, and Tony was sure that Susan had protected them by telling them only that she had to go away. She had been generous to a fault by leaving each member of her staff a check. Having been brought up into a family of *fides punica*, Tony did not have ordinary feelings of affection for people, much less understand such sentiments. Even that special love felt for infants was short-lived. People were to be controlled by fear and money, therefore, money was removed from his safe and sent in two separate packets to the relative's home. One packet was addressed to the contractor and contained the specifics of the job to be accomplished and the payment for such; the other was addressed to the relative and contained a *gift.* By Friday evening, the contractor had flown in from New Orleans, picked up his packet, and flown into Atlanta's Hartsfield Airport. Within four hours, he had rented a car and driven to Martinsville. Interestingly enough, as he had driven Interstate 75 north on the way to his destination, he would never have imagined that a wrecker from Tennessee traveling Interstate 75 south, pulling a car rented by the missing man Pinkie, passed him on the way down to Atlanta.

Dominic Cheves didn't like the idea of the new job he was assigned. The big cities might have an up to date police force which made it more difficult to escape if you were somehow caught doing a job, but if you were any good at all, you weren't caught. Small towns usually had rinky-dink law enforcement, but a stranger stood out like a man in purple tights. It was not his decision to be here. His boss owed a favor and he was told, not asked. Dominic drove through the town, then turned around and went back, driving left then right in a random fashion. He finally spotted the Day's Rest and parked in front of the unit that had a sign that read **Resident Manager**.

Dominic got out and went in, rang a bell and waited a few minutes until a man who was obviously a drinker appeared. The man had a days stubble on his face, red bloodshot eyes, and a voice that sounded like a foghorn. "What can I do for you?" Dominic was not high on the totem of good looks and squeaky clean hygiene, but he was about three levels above the manager's regulars, and when Dominic spoke, he did so with the assurance of a man who was accustomed to having people take him seriously. "I want a room for a week to ten days, *hot* water for showers, clean sheets every day, and a TV that works. Got it?" The manager was not accustomed to anyone *this* aggressive, but answered quickly, "Yeh."

"How much?" Dominic asked. The manager coughed, put his hand over his mouth, and answered, "Uh, two hundred seventy-five a week." Domino knew the type, but didn't quibble, "Find me a girl to give me a massage, and I'll pay you three hundred." Then, as if it were of no real concern, he added, "I'm expecting an associate from out of town. He and I are going to be looking at property. His name is Dirk Miese." The manager did not want to sully this deal, so kept quiet about the man in Unit 10. Tomorrow would be soon enough to tell this man that he thought the man Dirk Miece had checked out yesterday. The manager had a habit of keeping an eye out for potential marks that he could filch off of when they left their room. Last night had been an unusually boisterous one at the Day's Rest. One of the men had holed up in one of the rooms with a gal he saw periodically. The man's wife had shown up around two thirty in the morning and had caused a ruckus. The manager had to threaten to call the police (which he had no intention of doing) before he could get the man to go home with his wife who was trying to beat up the gal. The manager had no sooner gotten rid of them and crawled back in bed, when he heard something. Looking out the window, he saw a wrecker pulling Mr. Miece's car away.

Today, there was no activity in unit 10. He watched the unit earlier, and finally checked inside. It was empty. Even the ashtrays, glasses, and remote control looked clean. Someone had wiped the room with care. The manager wished he had written down the name (did it have one?) of the wrecker company. If he had gotten the license tag number, there might have been a bonus to be made. As if was, the only way to make a buck off of this dude was to string him along for a day or two. Meanwhile he would take care of the man's bodily needs. Deanna would do nicely. *The locals liked her massage.* He thought about putting the man in Unit 10, now that it was clean, but he couldn't be sure the man, Miece, wouldn't come back. He finally decided to put the man up in Unit 6. There had been a fire in it a month ago. The insurance had paid for renovating the room, and it had new furniture. He had been saving it for some high-class traveler, but this guy looked like he might not appreciate the level of cleanliness in the other Units, even if he looked a little rough around the edges. He handed the key to Dominic, who gave the manager two one hundred dollar bills and told him, "Here's two bills. One is an advance on the room. If everything is clean and you give me good service, I'll give you the two hundred more tomorrow. Meanwhile, the other bill is for three things: information, a bottle of Tequila, and the girl. I'll pay the girl myself for her services. You just make sure all three of those things are the best."

Before the man could turn and leave, the manager stopped him. "Sir," he said he a cowed voice, "You haven't signed the register." "Sure I did," Dominic said in a surly tone. You just spilled something on it and can't make it out." With that, he turned and left the office. The manager stood watching the back of this—real estate speculator? Mobster? Killer?—retreating, and thought back to a time when he was a young man and very cocky. He had lived out in Dallas, Texas at that time. He got mixed up with some big-time goons that would just as well blow you away as look at you. They had given him three hundred bucks to kill a man. He couldn't do it. He sneaked out of town, hitch-hiked to Atlanta. He spent the money for room and board, looked over his shoulder until he was ready to give up, but finally pulled himself together and caught a ride with a truck driver who just wanted someone along for company. When they got to Martinsville, he pretended he lived there and asked to be dropped off. That was thirty years ago, and the man who had just left and the man who had been in Unit 10 were the same type as those men in Dallas. Killers. But what were they doing in Martinsville? The manager's name was Roy, and Roy wanted them gone. He had been guilty of nickel and dime crap, but these guys were out of his league and he wanted them as far away from his motel as possible. He ran a good establishment that filled a need, and he didn't want anyone causing the law to come snooping around his place. In the morning he would tell the man that he had been off-duty when this Miece had checked in, and the man had left without even turning in the key. That way, he'd be at least a hundred bucks or so to the good, and the guy would leave town. Feeling a little more in control of the situation, Roy called Deanna. *The man in Unit 6 didn't have to know that the girls usually paid Roy a referral fee.*

~ 14 ~

Susan lounged in bed on Sunday morning, experiencing languor from both the physical and mental activities of the previous night. She had not danced that much since her college days; and the emotional stir she apparently created was not what she had anticipated. The realization that she had to quickly replace her image of a femme fatal prompted her to sit up and throw her feet over the side of the bed. At that moment, hearing a knock at the door, she grabbed her robe and pulled it on as she walked uncertainly over to the door and opened it slightly. Jay stood there with a grin on his face. In his hand was one of the shoes Susan had worn the night before. Susan had not been accustomed to wearing high heels for long periods of time, much less, dancing for hours in them. Last night she had taken them off in the car on the way home.

Jay's personality had many facets, and now another emerged when he said very seriously, "I'm wondering if you've lost anything else. Might prove to be embarrassing later on. Should I go outside and look in the shrubbery?" Susan looked at the shoe and answered, "I don't think the prince in Cinderella was this suggestive." Jay's eye brow went up and a hint of a smile flashed across his face as he answered, "But Cinderella wasn't Irish."

"And what does her ancestry have to do with it?" she asked, searching his face for some clue to what he was up to. "Well, to tell the truth, I was trying to get your Irish up before suggesting that if you wish to accompany Julia to church this morning, you might try to look just a little frumpy. Remember, to look as good as you do is a sin in itself."

Susan was again caught in the paradox of his rhetoric. "No," she said.

"My dear lady," he countered, "This is not your slipper?" "No, no, no," she said. "I didn't mean no to that!" Now Jay was going into his lawyer mode, enjoying Susan's discomfiture. "Just what were you saying no to then?" he asked.

"Jay, never mind." she answered, feeling the tantalizing power he had with words.

"So," he continued, "Are you the owner of this slipper?"

"Yes," she answered.

"Good," he said, "Because I have just twenty minutes before I'm due at church. I'm on usher duty today."

"Oh!" Susan exclaimed, as she looked at her watch, "Go, I have to dress." As she closed the door in his face, Susan heard Jay say, "Julia said that she'll have the car ready and drive the two of you. Try to find your ugliest dress, and don't wear any lipstick. You'll have to go easy until their jealousy wears off. They'll discover that in addition to being beautiful, and a great dancer, you are also tremendously talented, above average in intellect, and a wonderful cook. There! Did I leave anything out?"

Susan was in the shower and not listening, however, when Jay, laughing, turned to leave; Julia stood in the hallway, watching him and shaking her head as she said, "You are so much like my father, it's like seeing him again. Don't worry her, Jay. She'll soon have the town cheering for her. I'm grateful that I wasn't beautiful. I think it's a burden."

"But you're wrong," He said, "Not only were you beautiful as a young woman, you're beautiful right now. And I don't think Susan's going to worry about anything except doing the right thing. I imagine you were the same way when you were her age, and as for me, I am the happiest of men." He turned then and left, saying, as he walked away, "But do tell her if she can sing, to try singing a little off key. At least until people gets to know her."

Julia knew that Jay understood that she had not arrived at her position in the town through wealth. People were sometimes as unforgiving of people with wealth as much as they were of those with strength and talent, and she had grown from a child into a woman with all three. She had to work twice as hard as anyone else, doing twice as much in the church and community and still endure twice as much criticism as anyone else before her reputation was established. Julia watched with pride as Jay left, knowing that he appreciated the responsibility that came with having wealth, intellect, and talent. She then went back to the breakfast room to finish reading her paper.

One of the items in the Martinville Gazette that had troubled her, under a sort of gossip column called **Gazing & Phrasing**, was mention (from an undisclosed source) of land speculators that were looking for land to buy in the area. The Martins were probably the largest land owners in the town. But land was not just a commodity to the Martins and never had been. Stocks and Bonds were impersonal, but not land. Land was a legacy that had been passed down from generation to generation in their family. There were buildings built by various members of the family that were landmarks. There were schools and streets named for long gone members of both the Prescott and Martins, as well as other pioneers. The pride in the town was shared by most of the people who wanted the integrity of Martinsville to continue so they could raise their children without the corrupting influences found in larger cities, and money was not the most important thing to them. Julia wanted to maintain the innocence of the town. Speculators wanted to make money.

Julia became aware that Susan was speaking to her, "I hope I'm not making you late, Julia." Julia looked at her watch. It was twelve minutes before eleven. "No, of course not," she said, "You look very nice, Susan. I hope you'll forgive Jay's teasing. My father was a terrible tease. A good man, but a tease none the less. Of course my mother thought that he taught me not to take myself too seriously, and she was probably right. If you're ready, we'll go."

During the five minute drive to church, Julia told Susan that after lunch she would drive out and visit Ralph Getz's wife. The poor woman could not be persuaded to join in any activities, civic or church, and Julia suspected that Ralph abused her. As long as he didn't know when Julia would be making one of her surprise visits, he was afraid to do anything that would leave bruises on his wife. Julia usually took her some little something and stayed for about forty-five minutes to an hour. The woman's name was Vera. "Vera," Susan said. "How ironic."

"I know," mused Julia, remembering Vera's reaction when told what her name meant in Latin—truth. Julia had gotten Vera started reading the Bible and several months later Vera had read her the verse where St. Paul had said, "And you shall know the truth and the truth shall make you free.". Vera had asked Julia, "Is it really true that knowing the truth will make you free.?" Julia told Vera, "Yes," but knew Vera would require a lot of counseling before she would be free.

Vera had been uncomfortable with Julia at first but later warmed up to her generosity as she accepted magazines and books Julia brought her. Also, Vera realized that although Ralph tried to force her to discourage Julia, Julia refused to stay away and that had eliminated the beatings.

When Julia and Susan walked into the church, Jay made a point of escorting them to the Martin Family pew. Most of the time, people honored her by leaving the place vacant, even when she was not there. Today as Jay seated the women, he was unusually austere, and Susan was grateful. She had picked out a cream colored dress with a blouson top and a full skirted bottom that disguised her body in the folds of yards of soft flowing material. With the exception of a pale lipstick, she wore no color. Even Quakers wouldn't have found fault with her attire. The only bad moment came when Jay was standing near her while the collection plate was passed. He winked at her! She looked straight ahead, feeling the color rise to her face as her eyes locked for a moment with the minister's who was sitting in the chair next to the podium right in front of her. He politely averted his glance. There was an older woman with a beautiful contralto voice singing "Precious Memories."

At the end of the service, Jay introduced Susan to the minister as his fiancée. The minister was gracious, congratulating Jay and giving best wishes to Susan, asking if they had set a date. Susan was now officially engaged, ring or not. As she left the church on Jay's right arm with Julia on his left, she felt so completely fulfilled that if at that moment the earth had ended, she would have died happy. On the way *home*, she chided herself silently for allowing the fear that this was not real to occasionally slip into her mind and mar the happiness that flowed through her like a transcendental experience. *I must learn to accept love for what it is.*

~ 15 ~

On Monday morning by ten o'clock, Jay and Susan had arranged their affairs so they could be away for a couple of days; Jay postponing appointments, Susan deferring any decisions for another day. Their plan was to meet with Bruce Nesmith at one-thirty at the Richard Russell Building in Atlanta and then spend the rest of the time shopping. They were booked at the Ritz Carlton with separate rooms. Jay was the epitome of propriety. They would spend the night, which included dinner at Nicholai's On the Roof, and take in a show later in the evening. Bruce had arranged everything. The ride to Atlanta was comfortable. Susan and Jay talked seriously about their future. He asked her what she thought about remaining in the family home. Susan said she saw no reason to live elsewhere if Julia was agreeable. She told him she wasn't planning any changes regarding her business plans, and he agreed that she should have the right to a career. At that point, however, he reached over and took her hand and told her in a solemnly teasing voice, "You must remember that you have an obligation to satisfy this beast that you have awakened in my sleeping libido. And, eventually, of course, that means babies and diapers and formula and etcetera, etcetera." Susan basked in the feel of his hand squeezing hers. His hands were the most wonderful combination of warm, smooth flesh covering firm muscle.

"So you're saying I'm supposed to arrange my catering business around catering to your monkey business?" she playfully asked.

"Well, well, well," Jay quipped, "The lady thinks our amorous tryst is "monkey business'?"

Susan laughed and squeezed his hand before saying. "I don't think my lord is going to lack for plenty of love-making. And as for babies, etcetera, etcetera, I think I'll have plenty of help." Both seemed to be satisfied with the other's response as they rode for the rest of the trip silently relishing the prospects of their future life together. They continued to hold hands until the traffic required Jay to release Susan's hand and place it on the steering wheel. Romance is something that remains in a person's imagination, no matter the age, and Jay and Susan had not avoided marriage before; they had simply waited for the right person.

When they arrived at the Ritz Carlton, Jay requested a tray of salad and sandwiches to be sent to his room. By the time Susan and Jay were settled in their rooms, the order arrived and a light lunch was enjoyed by the two before time to go for the interview with the FBI. The hotel accommodations were resplendent with luxuriant carpets, wall treatments, and every possible visual means that blatantly, but silently stated, "We are the finest!" Susan was not one to avoid competition if necessary, but it occurred to her that to survive as a caterer in a large city that drew its share of convention trade, as Atlanta was known for, would be no less than a sixty hour a week enterprise—no time for monkey business or babies in that arena! Her thoughts lingered on the *babies* aspect of her revelry, and she suddenly realized that, although she had always assumed she would have children when she married, she had never *really thought about it until now.* She had just finished refreshing her makeup in the bathroom when she heard Jay's knock. He asked as she opened the door, "Are you about ready?"

"Yes," she answered and then abruptly turned and went back to the bathroom before picking up her purse, fearful he would see what she saw as she looked in the mirror at her flushed face. *The thought of Jay's previous love-making had pervaded her thoughts and she could not avoid the images that made a simple touch of his hand suffuse her with desire. She dampened a wash cloth with cold water and gently pressed it against the back of her neck and face.* When she returned, she avoided Jay's glance, fearing he could read her thoughts. This Mr. Nesmith was expecting them at the Bureau!

The trip through downtown Atlanta by way of Peachtree Street was wonderful. The famous Dogwoods were in bloom, and the eclectic mix of Old South antebellum homes interspersed with twentieth century storefronts in the outer part of the city was charming. The modern skyscrapers in the center of town, accentuated by a beautiful blue sky as a background gave a view of the best of the old and new.

Susan had felt no sense of foreboding until she saw the almost antiseptic glare of the sun shining on the vast array of white granite buildings with the stately but austere Russell Building nestled in their midst. As they turned toward the parking facility, Georgia's state capital building dome covered with gold from the mines of Dahlonega glistened like a palace.

After they had parked and approached the entrance to the FBI headquarters, she found her throat was dry and a faint chill swept through her entire body. Jay reached out and took her hand as if sensing her change of mood. He was accustomed to the detection devices in the lobby and guards wearing pistols and grim faces. Susan was asked to surrender her purse to the conveyor belt as she walked through the electronic point-check. Suddenly, everything was stopped and two guards stopped her as she reached to retrieve her purse. "Ma'm," the older man said with a strident tone, "We detect a knife in your handbag." Susan was startled. Her mind tried to imagine what on earth this man was talking about. "No," she said, "I don't carry knives," and the need to relieve the tension was so great that she nearly added, "Except in my kitchen." She looked at the viewer that the guard showed her as he asked, "And what is that?" Susan was so unnerved by the procedure that she forced herself to reply in the softest possible voice, "If you open my purse and take it out, I think you will find that to be a nail file," then realizing that the men were just doing their duty and needed to save face, she added, "I'm sorry officer, I just didn't think to check my purse." The guard was appeased by her accepting blame for the incident and let her go on while Jay was soon right behind her.

He slipped his arm around her waist. Not one to lose an opportunity to use his dry wit, he pulled her slightly into him as he quipped, "You had me worried for a minute. I thought for sure I was escorting a beautiful terrorist who was just using my heart and body to her advantage. I'm relieved. You really *do* love me?" At moments like this, if Susan had any doubts that Jay Martin was *the* man for her, those doubts were quickly dispelled. She laughed as they approached the elevator, vaguely aware that the three men waiting there were staring at her and Jay. He whispered in her ear before they reached the elevator, "I love you too." Self-conscious as if they were observing two lovers through a keyhole, the men turned away.

They found Bruce's office and, as soon as they spoke to his receptionist, he came out, greeted them, and took them into his office. Bruce's eyes left Susan only for a moment as he bid a cursory greeting to Jay. He and Jay had always been friendly because of the relationship between their mothers but had never considered themselves friends in the true sense of the word. Bruce was a perfect candidate for the FBI. He was an organization man who would do as directed by his superiors, while at the same time forever trolling the political waters of the organization, looking for any opportunity that would forward his advancement. Jay, while able to surround himself with competent personnel and imbue his staff with loyalty, was a loner. He respected and rewarded his staff for their hard work and loyalty, but there was never any doubt in anyone's mind that Jay ran the show. In fact, Jay's occasional diffident behavior in court was not a reality but an act of savoir-faire put on for the benefit of a judge that might otherwise be intimidated by his prodigious knowledge of the law.

As Jay stepped forward and shook Bruce's hand, he noted that *that* was the only time Bruce took his eyes off Susan and knew if the two men's roles were reversed, he would do the same. Bruce explained that he was not the one who would conduct the interrogation—it was not his job, nor would it be professionally wise in view of his and Jay's personal relationship. Relishing Bruce's captivation with Susan, Jay was amused as Bruce sought to detain them as long as possible by engaging in chit chat, but when he saw that the appointment with the jeweler might have to be delayed until tomorrow, his patience evaporated.

"Bruce," he interjected, "How long will it take for Susan's interview. I just realized that time is getting away from us and we have another appointment at three-thirty." For a moment Bruce looked as though cold water had caught him full face, but he quickly rallied and said, "I'm sorry, of course you have other things planned. It's just that we see each other so infrequently, I seem to have turned a business call into a social one. I'll walk the two of you down to the office where the affidavite will be conducted." When the two men stood up and shook hands, Bruce uttered sotto voce, "You're a lucky devil." The two men's eyes met in complete understanding.

There was one awkward moment when they stepped out into the hall. It was obvious that all three could not possibly walk down the hall, so Jay allowed Bruce one last sip of the elixir he had become drunk on for the past thirty minutes. "Bruce," he asked, "Why don't you walk Susan on down to the room and I' ll join her in a few minutes. The men's room is this way?" Bruce, pleased, smiled and said, "Righto."

The questions asked by the Bureau were noninvasive. In fact, Jay decided that they had already learned the truth about Susan's character and lack of involvement with Vascola's organization from various friends and business associates of Susan's. There were verifications that she had been stalked by this Tony Vascola, and her staff would have known that she was avoiding him. They must have been shocked by her sudden departure, but undoubtedly she had left them a sizable severance check. The Bureau had gained access to her bank records and had satisfied any question of her benefiting from the mob's operation. In addition, the Bureau had also tracked where Susan had disposed of her car by trade.

The interrogation was conducted and an affidavit signed within a little over an hour. Jay had kept quiet except for a rare occasion when Susan was confused by the way a question was worded. The agents seemed to be satisfied with the answers both Susan and Jay supplied. While Bruce Nesmith was not involved in the prceedings, his clout at the Bureau and his relationship with the Martins was of inestimable value.

As they emerged from the Russell Building, Jay leaned over and kissed Susan. It was a brief kiss meant to encourage her after what he knew to be an unpleasant culmination to a too long endured disruptive and frightening affair. The jeweler they had an appointment with was located in Lenox Square, a large and sprawling shopping center located less than five miles from downtown Atlanta and down the street from the Ritz Carlton. They were on time for the appointment, and within half an hour of viewing rings, Susan found one that both she and Jay liked. The ring was too large, so it was decided that a guard would be attached until the ring could be sized in Martinsville.

By six o'clock they were back at the Ritz Carlton where Jay ordered a bottle of champagne to be sent to their room and arranged for a limousine for their drive to Nikolais later. Afterwards, each retreated to separate rooms. Susan had taken a hot shower and was coming out of her bathroom, when she became aware of a soft knocking at her door. She quickly slipped on her robe and after securing the sash, opened the door with the chain still on. There was a cart outside with a bottle of champagne and glasses. Jay stood beside the cart with *that* eyebrow raised looking at the door. She released the chain and opened the door as he said. "Room service."

Once he was in the room, he closed the door and took her in his arms. "I said I would not touch you again until I had put a ring on your finger. Now, what do you say to that?" Susan untied her sash and asked, "What took you so long?"

~ 16 ~

When Jay awakened on Tuesday morning, he slowly rolled out of bed and stretched. Susan was sleeping soundly, her hand tucked under his pillow as though seeking to stay connected, while simultaneously allowing him freedom of movement. He watched the rise and fall of the coverlet as she breathed and thought of his incredible luck that so long ago, this remarkable person and her father had just happened to drive through Martinsville and been impressed with the town enough to come back years later. Even though Tony Vascola was a scoundrel, Jay could not but have some small regard for the man that had driven Susan straight into his arms. *Well, not quite so . . . . Julia Martin was, as always, the queen of sages. recognizing Susan's character and bringing her into their home.*

Susan's eyes opened and she smiled at Jay, remembering the total abandonment of their previous night's love-making. "Don't give me that enchantress smile," he said in mock sternness. "You've worn me out. I am a mere shadow of my former self." Susan laughed in delight at his taciturn way of communicating his satisfaction with their night's union. He leaned over and kissed her, then found himself caught up in the perfume of her body, her warmth, and a passionate urgency as she pulled him to her. *Breakfast and shopping could wait!*

By ten o'clock, the couple's ardor satiated—at least to the point that they could remember they had obligations that had to be fulfilled back in

Martinsville—they took leave of the conjugal bed. They, however, made the mistake of taking a shower together and the journey home was postponed for another hour. When they emerged from the Ritz Carlton after an early lunch, they decided to go back to Lenox Square for a quick trip through Neiman Marcus. Everywhere they went, people seemed to be staring at them. Susan was not feeling the least bit guilty, so she could not attribute the attention due to *that* type of self-conscious penitence but thought it more like the attention of the main figures in an old-fashioned musical. *Funny!*

Walking through the mall, they stopped in front of a store window that had a mirror in the display. Looking at her reflection, Jay squeezed Susan's hand as he said, "Are you aware of how absolutely radiant you are? People are staring. You're beautiful." Susan was a little embarrassed at being called beautiful but somewhat relieved to know what was causing the stares. Ironically, two months ago when she looked at herself in the mirror while in West Palm, she had almost cried at what she saw. Her skin was pale and there were circles around her eyes. That's over now! *I'm in love and I feel beautiful!*

Julia had suggested that if they found anything they felt she couldn't do without to buy it. Both Julia and Jay were so loyal to the shopkeepers in Martinsville, they usually just looked and then went home and had any items they wanted ordered. through local merchants. There was one thing, however, that Susan insisted on purchasing—a wonderful deal on one of her favorite wines. By the time she had finished ordering the wine, Jay handed over his credit card to the clerk and Susan allowed the transaction to take place. Leaving the mall after this incident, Susan thought about the time she and her father had flown a beautiful Chinese kite at the beach on a windy day. The wind had caught the kite and taken it high in the air so that she was battling to keep it from pulling out of her hands. Her father said, "Let it go sweetie. I know you love the kite and want to keep it, but you have to know when to let go of things." Her father's words were ostensibly about the kite, but as time went by, Susan thought about that day on the beach and came to understand that he was talking about far more than the kite.

The couple started the ride back with the knowledge that the bittersweet finish of the trip was just something to overcome for now. Neither had any doubts of their future together. Susan had a great respect for adhering to legal means of binding contracts, but felt in her heart that she married Jay *that night* four days ago. What she would have loved was to stay in Atlanta or anywhere with Jay—the traditional honeymoon. She was not ready to get back to work. When she was in high school and college, she had known girls that had *gone all the way*. There seemed to be more who had a carefree idea about sex than the opposite attitude. Susan had never met anyone that she cared enough about to violate her father's trust. He had been a great father. He never seemed embarrassed to talk about such things with her. After her mother died, he told her she was the most precious thing in his life, and he wanted her to know a man would quite often say anything to lure a girl into having sex with him, but if he were really the type of man that she would want to spend the rest of her life with, he would never pressure her or seduce her.

Susan tried not to be judgmental about the constant parade of men her college room-mate seemed to fall in and out of love with, and most of all she always found ways to avoid discussing these things or going out with buddies of her room-mate's current love. She would offer all kinds of excuses and spent most of her time in the library studying to get away from the hassle. That seemed so long ago. She thought of a record that her room-mate used to play until it got on her nerves, but now she felt the words. *I need love, love, love. Yeah!*

The ride back to Martinsville was quiet with Susan and Jay lost in their own private thoughts that occasionally splashed over on the other with a demonstration of affection by a touch or a momentary squeeze of one another's hand. Susan thought of the difference between Tony Vascola and Jay. Tony's personality was a veneer of gallantry concealing a ruthless ego. Jay's taciturn demeanor soon dissolved to reveal a man of wit, affection, and honor. Jay's squeeze of her hand brought Susan back to the present. She realized they were not more than a half hour from home. The thought of going back to their former routine sent a wave of tension throughout her body. Jay felt the change in her immediately. "What's wrong?" he asked.

"It suddenly occurred to me that we are going to have to go back to our former routine," she replied with a slight tremor in her voice. Jay squeezed her hand and answered in his softest voice, "My mother has waited a long time for grandchildren. We can have a simple wedding ceremony with a few friends within the next day if necessary, or we can take a month to plan a grand wedding and invite all the town-folks. It's your choice. However, you are now my bride, with or without a ceremony, and I gaurantee unless you lock your door, I will sleep in your bed."

Susan was suddenly thrust back into her former traditional thinking. "And how about Julia?" She asked. Without the slightest hint of humor, Jay replied, "Julia and I are close, but she'll sleep in her own bed." An exasperated Susan squeezed Jay's hand and cried, "You are maddening!"

"Mad about you, but don't break the hand that's planning to caress you tonight," Jay answered as he felt Susan's emotion in her grip. Then he continued, "Julia is a mature, God-fearing woman who has read the Bible at least a dozen times in her life. Think of her as Naomi, you are Ruth and I am Boaz. Okay?" Susan rode in silence, ashamed to admit to Jay that she had only a vague idea of what he was talking about. Ruth and Naomi rang a bell, but youth Bible study hadn't been a high priority for her church and college only covered the high spots. Apparently the answer could be found in the Bible and there was one on her dresser where it had remained after she moved in. "Okay," she said, but she was not sure.

Susan's thoughts returned to Tony Vascola. When she left Florida, she was hoping to get away from him and establish herself in the small town of Martinsville. Just to have accomplished that would have made life rewarding again, but now her future with a man like Jay was something that only happened in movies. And to have a mother-in-law, no—a mother like Julia was miraculous. Susan still found it hard to believe that she had outsmarted Tony. The FBI had found her, so why not Tony? Did her testimony yesterday sever her future connection to him, or would he somehow find out her whereabouts through his lawyers? She shuddered at the thought.

"Okay, what's fermenting in that beautiful Irish head of yours?" Jay's question came without any warning and Susan was not sure how to answer. She wasn't accustomed to lying, *but is honesty always the best policy*? She felt confused.

"Jay, I not only love you, I love Julia. But I feel as though I have involved you both in something that you may regret. What if the FBI divulges to Tony Vascola's lawyers my whereabouts? What if he sends someone to Martinsville to cause trouble or try to force me to go back to Florida? Everything has happened so fast. I'm sure that what I feel is not a flight of fancy. I've never had an image of someone that would be *Mr. Right*, but I never doubted that I would know when he came along. But how about the people in Martinsville? What would happen if my connection to Tony Vascola were known? Look at it the way the townspeople would look at it: This *femme fatale* comes to town, talks Julia into renting out a room in her home, ingratiates herself into Julia's trust, and then seduces you. And to add complete credibility to the whole scenario-I'm—she's a gun moll!"

Jay's response was totally unexpected. He started laughing. At first Susan thought he was clearing his throat. The sound then rolled out into a full belly laugh. She was dismayed. She had never heard Jay do any more than chuckle. She put her hand on the car handle and with a trembling voice requested, "Stop, and let me out."

Jay's response was well thought out before he said anything. He ignored her request and drove a good five miles before he spoke. Susan was furious—he could hear her breathing as if trying to catch her breath. Finally he said, "I'm sorry for my total lack of sensitivity to what I now realize is a real fear to you. What I should have done was to allay your fears by assuring you that the people in Martinsville would never assume that Julia could be taken in by subterfuge by anyone; and as for me being seduced, if they thought it were really true, they would revel that a woman had finally brought me to my knees. And as far as this scoundrel coming to Martinsville, let him dare! Either his henchmen or himself. You do yourself an injustice to think that way." When he had finished speaking, Jay listened for any sounds that would indicate Susan's mood.

Tentatively he reached for her hand and squeezed it. The moisture told him he had caused her to cry. "Susan, you are going to have to be patient with me. My mother puts up with me because she's my mother. One day I hope you and I will have a son and then you'll put up with him, but I was a jerk to laugh at your fears. Believe me when I say I just can't imagine why you should be afraid. Neither Julia nor I are fools. You are so much more than you imagine yourself to be." Susan moved over next to Jay and put her head on his shoulder. Jay pulled her as close to him as possible. "Better?" he asked.

"Yes, but I'm embarrassed. I sounded like a frightened school girl. I really don't blame you for laughing. And you're right about you and Julia—you're both smart, no not just smart—you're wise people. I think more than being afraid of Tony Vascola, I'm really afraid that I'm going to suddenly have my wonderful dream turn into a nightmare. I don't know what I would do if I lost you or Julia." By this time they were in the outskirts of Martinsville and instead of going home, Jay drove past his street and into the court house parking lot where he parked and told Susan, "I'll be back in a few minutes." Ten minutes later he was back with a piece of paper in his hand.

"Did you go to Atlanta with unfinished business?" she asked. "Nope. Well yeh," he answered after he thought a second.

The next stop he made was at the back of Dr. James office. "Okay, sweet lady. You and I are going to have blood tests done." "Jay?" Susan asked as though all her doubts were compacted into that one syllable. "Come," was all he said. Susan got out of the car and followed Jay into the back door of the office.

~ 17 ~

Apparently Jay had called the doctor's office from the courthouse. A nurse was waiting and, as if such things happened routinely, took blood from Susan and Jay. The doctor interrupted his last scheduled visits long enough to congratulate Jay and wish Susan the best, then winked at Jay as Susan turned to go. "I always knew you were smart," he told Jay, "Now I know you're damn lucky too!" Susan went quickly through the side exit and got in Jay's car, pretending she hadn't overheard the doctor's remark. Atlanta had been wonderful, even with the FBI interrogation. *Now I feel like I'm back in a gold fish bowl!* Jay, following close behind, slipped into the driver's seat humming the bridal march. He reached over pulling Susan into his arms, and said before he kissed her, "Mark has asked me a dozen times over the years what I was saving myself for. Today I showed him." Susan had always had her share of attention. However, in a city such as West Palm Beach where the wealthy congregated, that also meant beautiful women were in large supply. These women thought nothing of spending thousands of dollars on plastic surgery, botox, and daily beauty aids. Susan was just one of many. What she wanted now was to marry Jay and get on with her career and be accepted for who she was. *Please forget my looks!*

As Jay and Susan pulled into the driveway at home, Julia was finishing the preparation of the evening meal, and when Jay and Susan opened the front door, the wonderful aroma of garlic and chicken pulled them into the kitchen where she was tossing a salad. "Well, you two are right on schedule," she said as she pushed the salad to one side and walked over to the two with out-stretched arms. She wrapped one arm around Susan and the other around Jay, kissing each in turn on the cheek. "You kids go wash up. I'll pour glasses of wine and we'll go out in the back and relax a little before we eat." Jay went out to the foyer where he had left their luggage, picked it up and carried it to their rooms. He brushed Susan's cheek with a kiss as he passed her in the hallway before disappearing into his room.

Susan went to her room, quickly stripped and put on light weight sweats, washed her hands and was out in the hall as Jay emerged in his sweats. They looked at one another and then laughed. Jay pulled Susan to him, kissed her long and passionately, pushed her back arms length and said, "I've never been addicted to anything in my life until now." With that said he put his arm around her shoulder and gently guided her to the back porch where Julia was waiting with wine.

As Julia was handing Susan her glass of wine, the beautiful solitaire caught her eye. "Excellent," she said. "I hope you'll forgive me for my bossiness, but you need to go down to Isacc Steine and have it sized and . . ." She didn't finish, suddenly aware that some time in the past two weeks the baton had passed from her hand to Susan's. Jay had been independent for years and she had just served as his personal secretary. Sort of a combination valet, chief cook and bottle washer. Old habits die hard, but she was an astute and generous woman. "Susan," she began again, "The ring is absolutely beautiful and suits you." Then she handed Jay's wine to him, picked up her own and raised her glass saying, "God bless you both. Now, tell me about your trip."

After relating the events of the trip to Julia and enjoying her sumptuous dinner, Jay and Susan retired for the night in separate bedrooms with the intention of catching up on their sleep before having to catch up on their work the next day. But after falling asleep immediately, Susan awoke a few hours later and couldn't go back to sleep. When three o'clock rolled over into four, she got dressed quietly, planning on working at her shop. She drove downtown and parked in front of her place, unlocked the door and was thrilled at the progress Frank Nigel and his crew had made. Wistfully, she thought of the ease of preparation it would take for the reception coming up—if the shop were finished. It would be a chore working out of Julia's kitchen. But . . . . *back to reality. Julia was a dear to offer her kitchen. The reception would be a wonderful introduction of her skills to the townspeople.*

Later, after going through some paperwork, she was inspecting everything when she heard a noise in the place next door that spooked her. Who, or what in the devil? Rats? First, she walked over to the inside wall and listened, trying to decide if she should get out of there; nixing that, she then walked over and made sure her front door was locked before placing her ear against the wall. There was a funny swishing noise as if someone were rubbing something back and forth. She tiptoed to the back door and carefully unbolted the lock, eased the door open and saw Ralph Getz's car parked next to the building. Her first reaction was one of relief, but then was quickly replaced by the question: *What in the name of Job was he doing next door with the lights out*? Susan didn't wait around to figure it out. She quickly went to the front door, let herself out, and was pulling out before Ralph saw the car leaving. Driving back home, she decided she would make it a policy in the future not to work at the shop alone, even in broad daylight!

When she pulled into the driveway, Jay was sitting on the front steps like a concerned father waiting for an errant adolescent to come home. Instead of questioning her though, "Good morning. Care to do a run with me?" was all he said. For a moment, Susan almost declined. Then changed her mind, asking, "Can you give me a minute to change my clothes?" "Absolutely," came back with a slight *chuckle.* This was the side of Jay that drove Susan crazy. She wasn't sure what she wanted to do, Slap him or kiss him. She went in and was back in less than five minutes. She had some toxins in her body screaming to be sweated out!

Breakfast consisted of blueberry bran muffins, yogurt, and coffee, graciously served by Julia when they got back from their run. Jay usually read the business section, then scanned the headlines for items that he felt warranted his attention. This morning he seemed to be looking rather than reading. Finally, Susan asked, "I perceive you have some unresolved problem on your mind." He slowly turned to look at her and queried, "Oh?" She pursued her probing. "Aren't you going to ask where I went this morning?" "Okay," he answered, laying down the paper, "Where did you go this morning?" "I went to the shop," she replied. "Well," he asked, "What do you think of what Frank has done so far?"

"It's looking great, Jay." At this point Susan couldn't continue the farce. "Jay, Ralph Getz was in that unit next door doing something with the lights out. I heard a noise and looked out the back and saw his car. I think he was in there when I pulled up in front and for some reason didn't hear my car. I don't ever want to be alone in the shop again." Jay replied, "Uh huh, especially at four o'clock in the morning." Susan was slightly taken aback. "How did you know the time?" she asked.

Jay took his last swallow of coffee, stood up and walked over and leaned down and kissed Susan on the forehead, then said, "First, I'm a light sleeper. Second, I happen to be an honorary deputy sheriff. But last, Larry Pitman called me to say he had been watching Ralph Getz's place when you pulled up to the building. He wondered if he should keep Ralph under surveillance or go in and talk to you." Susan, totally dismayed, asked, "Who in the world is Larry Pitman and why is Ralph Getz under surveillance?"

At this question Jay realized Susan was not to be deceived or placated by a weak explanation. "Okay, Susan. Larry Pittman is a police officer on the graveyard shift and Ralph Getz is believed to be involved in some shady business. I'm telling you this because you need to avoid being alone with Ralph and certainly not at four o'clock in the morning."

Susan was still not satisfied. "What was he doing?" Jay answered her, "I have no idea. We can't search his place without probable cause. People may think a small town has the clout outside the law but we don't do anything that isn't within the letter."

Susan started to speak, then stopped. As if reading her mind, he said, "I couldn't tell you without breaching police security. However, you have never been at risk. Larry was across the street and could have been there in a matter of seconds. In fact, when you went to the back door, he walked across the street. He stepped back in the shadows when you came out." Susan's face was pale and drawn as if she had been betrayed. She stood up, prepared to leave the breakfast area. Julia had left the room earlier when the disclosure had begun. Jay's realization that Susan felt that he had knowingly exposed her to a dangerous situation was upsetting. "I have known Ralph Getz for years. He is not a dangerous man. Merely a greedy and foolish man who occasionally steps outside the law. Mean, yes. But not dangerous."

Susan saw the pained look on Jay's face and was sorry she had overreacted. She reached out and placed her hand on his face and said, "I'm so sorry if I doubted you." Rather than reply, he took her in his arms and embraced her, burying his face in her hair, smelling her fragrance. They stood for a moment thus until he finally turned her face toward him and told her, "I don't think I would ever be the same again if anything happened to you. I didn't even know what I wanted until you came along." With that said, he turned and left.

Susan sat down at the table for a few minutes before going to her room where she fell on her bed. She wanted to cry but tears just wouldn't come. Instead she just lay and quietly moaned. She thought of a documentary she had watched years before of tribal women moaning over the death of a love one because they were forbidden to cry. *I hate to cry!* When she had finished, she could hear the faint noise of running water. *Thank God Jay was taking a shower and couldn't hear her wailing like an pubescent girl.*

~ 18 ~

Dominic had been soothed temporarily by the girl who came to his room last night, but now he had awakened in a dark mood. He had questioned the girl before she left early this morning. At first she had been evasive, giving him some bunk about not divulging information. He was glad he didn't have to hit her to get cooperation. He just took out his gun and started polishing it with the edge of the sheet. As she pulled on her tight skirt and top, she talked rapidly for a southerner. "I . . . I think I do remember now the man you're talking about. He drank Scotch. I hate Scotch. That was good Tequila you had last night. I'd never had a good brand like that before." Dominic waved the gun impatiently. "Cut out the crap. Tell me about the man!" Deanna was trembling as she put her shoes on. *Tell him, then get the hell out of here.* "He was pale like you say and I only saw him a couple of times. He had uhh . . . . problems, if you know what I mean. They get kinda mean when they're that way. But he just disappeared couple of days ago. I don't know nothing else to tell you."

Dominic pulled out some money and laid it on the bed. "You gotta number I can call you direct? I got business to take care of. Later I'll give you a call when I want you to come back" Deanna had picked up the bills and counted them with a mixed sense of fear and excitement. *Three hundred dollars! Fifty was the most she'd ever gotten.* "Anytime! Seven zero six three eight four eight four zero six," she answered, and just to make certain he didn't forget, she pulled a piece of paper and pen out of her purse and wrote the number down. She tried to get him to make eye contact before she left. He realized what she was doing, pointed the gun toward the door and said in a low voice, "Vamoose." *Hookers don't kiss on the mouth and hoods don't make eye contact!*

Dominic sat on the edge of the bed going over everything she and the guy on the front desk told him. The two accounts didn't match up and he was sure who was lying. But why did the desk clerk lie? That was the problem of having to operate in a little burg like this. In New Orleans or Atlanta he could use a little *friendly* persuasion on the man and he'd spill his guts without involving the cops. Here was a different system. Even a seedy motel like this had its proponents and the cops overlooked certain things as long as the higher ups tolerated the arrangement. *Money! He'd offer the man money!* He rubbed his hand across his whiskers and decided to find a barber shop and get a shave. He got out of bed, took a quick shower, dressed and went to the front office where the man looked up with a surprised, guarded look on his face. Dominic decided to try a more subtle approach: "Where can I find a barber shop that gives shaves?" The look of relief on the man's face was exactly what Dominic wanted, and he listened as directions were given. He then pulled a hundred dollar bill out of his billfold and laid it on the counter. When the man reached to pick it up, he slapped his hand on top of his and held it, saying, "Before you take my money, let's have a look at your registration book." Roy was caught. This was not someone to mess with. "Sure," was all he said as he pushed the book over with his free hand. Dominic released the man's hand and searched the book until he found the alias Pinkie had assumed. Out from the name was the license tag number and state. *Bingo!* Dominic resisted the urge to rip out the page and instead said, "Give me a piece of paper and pen." When he'd left, Roy reached under the counter and pulled out a bottle of whiskey and a shot glass, poured himself a drink and downed it. His hand was shaking, but not from DT's. The man who just left was out for blood and Roy didn't want it to be his!

After getting a shave and breakfast, Dominic called a contact in Atlanta who had insiders in various government facilities and were glad to earn a little money for passing information. The license tag number was traced and the vehicle was from a rental agency and had been returned. Dominic next called New Orleans and left a message to be passed on to Tony Vascola. Since Miece had evidently left his job unfinished, it was up to Dominic to take care of the *broad.* Knowing all of this didn't give him a lot of assurance.

It seemed like a great deal of trouble to go to for a dame that made you mad. Dominic's philosophy was very simple. If someone messed with you there were three choices: Ignore them, make um dead, or make um wish they were dead. It would be a lot easier just to take this woman out. He decided to carry on with the real estate farce as his cover, so spent the rest of the day driving around town, even out into the countryside. He had spotted Susan's shop. There was a sign being erected on the front of the building. He parked his car, walked over and tried the front door. Open. As he was walking in, two workmen looked up and then continued what they were doing. A redhead was over going through some boxes. When she looked up, Dominic knew this was the one. She was the kind of looker a man would do crazy things for. "May I help you?" she asked. For a moment Dominic was silent, then regaining his composure, he asked, "I'm looking for some property that's for sale. But I must have the wrong place." Susan had a strange foreboding about this man. She felt a slight chill when she realized why. He looked like he might be one of Tony's henchmen.

Susan shook off her fear and answered, "This building belongs to Ralph Getz. If you would like to talk to him I can give you his number." Dominic was now in the swing of his new identity. "Thank you. I appreciate that." This was a strange scene. Susan didn't believe the man was looking for real estate, and the man could almost feel the skepticism emanating from Susan, but each was committed to playing his or her polite role.

Susan walked over to her desk and pulled out one of Ralph Getz's cards and turned to walk over where the man was standing and nearly bumped into him. She suppressed a gasp and was glad she had made the decision not to stay in the shop alone. *The man didn't walk, he glided like some character out of a Alfred Hitchcock movie.*

"Here you are," Susan stated in her strongest tone. "Thank you," the stranger replied, then left.

Dominic sat in his car and awaited the little butterfly of doubt to land somewhere. The card with Ralph Getz name was still in his hand and he turned it over as he tried to piece together what could have happened to Pinkie, aka Miece. The butterfly disappeared and he resolved to forget Pinkie. Tony Vascola had a reputation for exacting his pound of flesh from anyone who displeased him. What he, Dominic, planned to do was to clean up the problem and get back to New Orleans.

He used his cell phone to call the number on the card and was immediately confronted with a "Yeh." Dominic wasn't one to stand on ceremony, but this was slightly abrasive even to him. "Ralph Getz?" Dominic asked. "Speaking," the voice tersely answered. Dominic didn't like the sound of the man and would have hung up except the idiot might call him back. "I'm looking for property for some investors and wondered if you knew of any for sale around this area." Ralph Getz's voice went from blatant indifference to rudely insinuating. "The people of Martinsville don't cotton to outside investors, Mr . . . . What did you say your name was?" "Smith," Dominic answered, then hung up. Dominic was not accustomed to being treated with disdain, at least not by hicks!

As soon as Dominic left Susan's shop, she made a telephone call to police headquarters and asked to speak to Officer Pitman and was told that he didn't come on duty until midnight. She thought of Officer Moore before she hung up and was told he was not in at that time. The dispatcher asked her, "If this is urgent I can reach him on his radio." "No," Susan replied, "I'll talk to him later." Her head was pounding and the dust had irritated her respiratory tract. She was searching in her purse for some ibuprofen, when she felt the *key*. It was the key to next door that Ralph Getz had forgotten to pick up. Her headache was pushed aside as a wild scheme popped into her mind. *I'm going next door!* The thought of anything beyond satisfying her curiosity never occurred to her. A plan was not as important as good timing, and the workmen being there gave her a sense of safety. She went out her back door, crossed over to the adjacent door, inserted the key, and as it turned, felt her stomach tighten. Hesitating just a moment, she then slipped through the door and closed it behind her.

The front windows had a wavy glass that prevented people from seeing in; however, light was ample. Dust and dirt covered the floor except where a pathway showing high traffic blazed a trail across the room. The trail led to the door of another room. She walked over to the door where a place on the old worn parquet flooring showed signs of something having been spilled and partially scrubbed up. Just as she reached out to try the door, it opened and Ralph Getz emerged! Susan almost cried out in fear. It was apparent he had heard her as he asked calmly, "Looking for something, Ms. Sullivan?" Susan took a deep breath and stepped back, still facing him, saying, "Yes, Mr. Getz. I'm glad you're here A . . . uh . . . . lot of my equipment has been installed and I'm not sure I'm going to have enough room. Perhaps I could rent this side too?" Ralph Getz was obviously agitated as he abruptly asked, "May I have my key?" He extended his hand, and as Susan handed the key to him, his hand grasped hers for a little longer than necessary. Whether it was intended as a sexual gesture or subtle intimidation didn't matter to Susan. The man was repugnant. Sensing her feelings toward him, he took great satisfaction in telling her, "I have a tenant for this side already. May not look like it to you, but he pays his rent and as long as he does that, he can let dust gather all he wants. That's his business!" Susan was slowly inching toward the back door. When she reached a point where she didn't feel hemmed in, she told him, "Well, I'm sorry if I invaded another tenant's space. I have to go. I have workmen next door and need to get over there. They'll be wondering about me." Susan turned and resisted the urge to run. She quickly left Ralph, crossed over to her back door, went in and locked the deadbolt.

The men were putting away their tools as she approached the work area. Still trembling, Susan grabbed her purse and waited at the front door as they left. The men nodded or tipped their hat to Susan but Mike was the only one who spoke to her, "Evening, Ms. Sullivan. See you tomorrow."

"Thanks Mike, you and your crew are doing a great job. Thanks again." As Susan walked out to her car, she tried to spot the police stakeout without being obvious. If one of the men was there, she couldn't spot him. She did see someone, however, who was definitely not looking for real estate. The man who had come in earlier and asked about property was sitting across the street under the shadow of a big oak at the edge of the church yard.

~ 19 ~

As Susan drove away from her shop, she thought of the kaleidoscope of events her life had encountered since leaving West Palm Beach. A vague sense of guilt still nibbled at her for ever having had anything to do with Tony Vascola. She had always prided herself in recognizing *that* kind of people. *Why did my intuition fail me?* Was the man back in the churchyard one of Tony's henchmen? Or could he be someone after Ralph Getz? Then she thought about the spot on the floor next door. That was what she had heard last night: the sound of someone scrubbing the floor. There was an old broom leaning against the wall. Her headache had returned. Or had it ever left?

She was glad to see the driveway and garage empty as she pulled in at the house on Main. *Good. I'll have a chance to get rid of some grime and this headache before Jay comes home.* What she needed was a long hot shower and some aspirin. The dirt, dust, and new paint had kicked up some allergies.

As Susan entered the foyer, the aroma of chicken and garlic was in the air. Curious, She went to the kitchen where a pan of Chicken Alfredo was sitting on the stove. Julia was nowhere in sight. Susan left the kitchen and retreated to her room. The shower felt wonderful as she stood with her head under the cascading hot water and scrubbed her body. The aspirin had started to take effect by the time she had dried her hair and rubbed herself with oil. Hearing a knock at the door, she slipped into a robe and opened her door slightly. Jay stood there with his eyebrow cocked, looking—wicked or mischievous?

"I'm not dressed," she told him.

"I don't mind," he quipped," But I just came to tell you that dinner will be served directly; however, if you care to have a drink, Julia and I will be waiting for you out back." Susan nodded, feeling slightly foolish.

When they had finished their drinks and shared the events of their day, Julia went to the kitchen, leaving the couple alone. Susan told Jay, "I had a strange man come into the shop today. He said he was looking for land for investors, but there was something unsavory about him that creeped me out."

"Why would he come into a catering shop to ask about land investment?"

"I don't know. He asked if the building was for sale. I thought perhaps Ralph Getz had planned to meet him there. When I realized he'd never heard of Getz, I gave him one of his cards. Later, when I left the shop, he was sitting in the shadows of that large oak tree across the street. I don't think someone looking to buy real estate sits in a parking lot and stalks potential sellers. If he was supposed to be watching someone, he wasn't doing a good job."

"What did he look like? Did you get his name?"

"No, I didn't get his name. He was either Hispanic or Mediterranean, five feet seven or eight."

"So, you spotted him but not Jerry Moore?"

"Yes . . . uh . . . No," Susan replied, relieved to know that Jerry was out there near by. Jay had become absorbed in his own private thoughts. After a couple of minutes he was about to say something when Julia came back and announced dinner. He shook his head as he got up and said. "Never mind."

Julia stood in the doorway waiting. "Okay, you two can't live on love, and my Alfredo has already suffered one of Henry's rampages this afternoon. I don't want to keep heating it."

After dinner, Susan told Julia, "I think your Alfredo would be good at any time, reheated or cold. I've never eaten anything you've cooked that wasn't delicious, so I'm just glad to know I won't be in competition with you in my catering business."

Julia stood up and began to clear away the dishes before she responded, "Susan dear, after all these years, I'm bound to have gotten it right. But thank you." Then she turned and walked away. Susan was surprised. This was not like Julia. Jay saw the dismayed look on Susan's face and explained, "Poor Julia. Henry must be really bad. She had to take him to the hospital this afternoon because Velma was a basket case and couldn't drive and keep him calm. After admitting Henry, the doctor insisted Velma be admitted too. She had been trying to handle Henry by herself. Julia said the doctor was afraid Velma was on the verge of a stroke."

Susan felt ashamed that she was not more sensitive to people around her. *I'm self absorbed.* "That's why she was gone when I came home?"

"Yes," Jay answered. There was a softness in his voice that Susan had heard only in their most intimate moments. "Velma and Henry were Julia's staunchest supporters when my father was dying of cancer. Now, Julia is determined to make everything as easy for Velma and Henry as possible." Susan stood up. Jay caught her hand.

"I need to help Julia," she protested.

"No." There was still a softness in his voice but now an added edge of firmness stopped Susan. "You're a sweet and caring woman," Jay told Susan, "But Julia needs to stay busy and grieve. Alone. And you and I need to sit out on the porch and plan our wedding." Susan had the same disoriented feeling she had when her father died.

Some people can be their best only when active. Susan felt powerless as she sat down next to Jay. He put his arm around her, pulled her to him and kissed her. She yielded to him at first, then started to pull away. "I haven't . . ." He didn't allow her to finish, just answered her, "I haven't either." Then kissed her again. When he finally released her, she told him, "But you didn't let me finish."

He replied, "I had garlic too. Everything can't be planned and squeaky clean. Did you mind my tasting of garlic?"

"No."

"Good, because not everything is perfect. Not everything can be fixed. When we marry, it will be for better or worse. You're beautiful. One day you may not be beautiful, but that's only part of the reason I love you. We may physically change, but I hope we'll always have this wonderful feeling about each other." They sat for a while just enjoying the closeness of their bodies touching side by side on the sofa, then Jay spoke in a rather solemn tone. "I want you to promise me not to allow yourself to be alone with any strangers. I have a uneasy feeling about what is going on in our placid little town. There's been some people new to this town asking questions, and that, coupled with Ralph Getz's activities leaves me troubled." Susan was a little surprised at Jay's concern. Although she was still edgy about the possibility of Tony's henchmen showing up, he had led her to believe Ralph Getz wasn't a problem. All in all she felt safe in Martinsville. She simply could not believe that bad things could happen to her in the sanctuary of her new adopted town. "You're really that concerned?" She asked.

"I'm not going to lose sleep, but I want you to be aware that you have the habit of judging people by standards that can't measure the unknown. My grandfather used to tell me that you can't tell by the looks of a frog how far he can jump."

"That was my father, Susan," Julia said as she came out on the porch. "He had a book of such homilies he loved to quote. I'm not going to disturb you two lovers, but I did want to pass along a couple of pieces of information. There has been some talk in town about land investors. No one seems to have a name of such a person or persons. Just rumor. With both Henry and Velma in the hospital, I may be busy and somewhat distracted in the days ahead. So Jay, you and Susan be my ears and eyes and bring this up at the next town council meeting. Okay? "Julia had walked over and stood in front of the couple. She leaned over and kissed her son and future daughter on the head then walked out of the room, her voice trailing as she did so, "I'm going to the hospital and will be back in an hour or so."

Jay turned to Susan and raised his eyebrow. "Your room or my room?" He asked. Susan had no qualms in Atlanta about her sexual tryst with Jay, but here, in the home of Julia gave her pause. "Jay, Julia may come back at any time." But even as she protested, Jay's hand was rubbing the back of her neck. His fingers felt *good!* He pulled back her hair and exposed her neck which he kissed. He then got up, gently pulled her to her feet, and led her through the house into the hall leading to their bedrooms. He hesitated at his door, Susan let out a sigh and pulled him into her bedroom.

As he closed the door behind him,. she stood with her back to him, suddenly shy . . . . at what? Rationally choosing to make love as opposed to yielding to passion? He walked up behind her and kissed her shoulder, then her neck as she flipped her hair back and turned. Her pulled the stretchy top and bra straps off of her shoulders, pulling them down and exposing her breasts. Her nipples were hard and pointed. He kissed her mouth first, then in turn each nipple, ending by running his tongue over them. She was unbuttoning his shirt, exposing his chest, and following his lead, ran her tongue over his nipples, gently biting each. He felt her body quiver as he ran his hand between her thighs, feeling the wetness. At that point it didn't matter whether Julia came home or not. There was an urgency in both Susan and Jay that couldn't be denied. They stopped the foreplay and quickly removed their clothes. As Susan pulled back the coverlet on the bed, Jay came up behind her and pressed himself against her. She felt the hardness of his groin and fell on the bed, turning as she did and pulling him into her as she opened her thighs. What happened next was indescribable. Their passion that had come to full dominion in Atlanta had been like a smoldering bed of coals ready to ignite. They both tried to hold back the erotic appetite that demanded consummation, but neither could stop the passion that ran like wildfire until it burned itself out. When it was over they lay in each others arms, Jay murmuring over and over again, "I love you, I love you," and Susan crying as if her heart was broken. When they were both spent and calm, Jay asked her, "Why did you cry? Was I all that bad?" Her laugh was so soft at first that he thought she had started to cry again. Then it soon escalated into the sound of a child being tickled and ended in a series of soft moans. He kissed her. "You are a crazy and wonderful woman. You know that don't you?"

Susan lay in Jay's arms for a while, just experiencing the warmth of his body, the musky masculine odor that was part of his unique identity, then reluctantly told him, "You need to go now before Julia comes home."

"Lovely woman, I am going to stay right here and hold you all night long. Julia will mind her own business and you and I are going to work on a future dynasty."

Susan just snuggled a little closer, knowing when she was bested.

~ 20 ~

The next morning Susan awakened to find Jay propped up on his elbow just watching her sleep. "So, do I snore?" She asked. "What man who's worth his salt would answer such a question," Jay said as he let out a yawn before continuing. "Besides, I can't be sure if I heard anything with my own snoring going on. He pulled her close to his chest and whispered, "Should we continue last night's frenzied activity or take a run?"

Susan lay cuddled in Jay's arms, but in her mind she was teetering between being the self-sufficient modern woman Jay knew her to be and the dependent child that seemed to have kicked in taking her totally by surprise. "No," she wanted to say. "I want to stay here and be warm and safe and loved and protected." Susan was nonplused by these foreign thoughts. The passion of her libido last night was now replaced by an overwhelming desire to stay where she was indefinitely. *So why couldn't she let go of the past and simply accept the here and now as real?* Jay felt the tension in her body and asked, "So, what's going on?"

Susan had berated herself many times for allowing herself to be deceived by Tony Vascola. She now understood completely. He had *protected* her from the thugs that had attacked her. The death of her father had left her feeling vulnerable. Even though she had always been independent, just knowing her father was there if she needed him had fed that independence. She was the high flying maid on the trapeze and he was her safety net.

Tony had the means of finding out everything there was to know about her and used that knowledge to his advantage. How was it that he had been at her shop at the exact time that she was attacked? *He had staged the whole thing!* She had avoided the intimacy that Tony kept pushing her toward, never feeling desire for him. *Thank you God. Thank you so much!* Susan rolled over and kissed Jay with such gusto it was his turn to be dismayed. "What is going on in that beautiful head of yours?"

Susan answered breathlessly as she rolled out of bed, "I'm just finding answers to some questions that have plagued me . . . and I love you very much. Let's go run." Suddenly feeling a little embarrassed at her nudity, she kept her back to Jay as she pulled her running shorts and top out of a drawer and slipped them on. Jay shook his head as he got out of bed. "Women. I think I need to read that book . . . uuhh . . . . something about men and women being from different planets."

When Susan and Jay returned from their long run, Julia had started breakfast, sending the aroma of hot coffee and fried ham wafting through the house. They went to their separate rooms to shower and dress, and trying to get the water temperature adjusted while showering, each laughed, realizing the competition that was now taking place. Ten minutes later, both entered the hall simultaneously. "Did you finally get your water temperature adjusted?" Susan asked. Jay cocked that devilish eyebrow and quipped, "I think you already know what the solution to that dilemma is." *Another cold shower!* Julia's appearance in the foyer ended further teasing. "Good morning you two. Coffee and ham are ready. How would you like your eggs? Poached, fried, or scrambled?" She seemed like her usual self and oblivious to Jay and Susan's activities the previous night. But what Susan didn't understand was that babies were on Julia's mind!

Susan turned the renovations to her shop completely over to Frank Nigel. Sometimes he was already working when she arrived; occasionally she opened. However, as the equipment came in, certain adjustments were inevitable before installation and only Susan could make those decisions. On this particular morning, neither Frank nor Mike were at the shop. There was the usual early morning traffic as people went to work but Susan was reluctant to open her shop alone. Jay's remark, intended for Susan's protection, had spooked her, and the thoughts of entering the dark shop filled her with dread. With the reception she was catering coming up in two days, she had to make the ingredients for the canapés tonight. Thank goodness the two large refrigerators had arrived. It had been sheer luck that the floor had been installed in time. Various recipes could be assembled in

Julia's kitchen and then transported to the refrigerators. Julia had located a used van for Susan at a very reasonable price. *Julia.*

As Susan sat in her car thinking about how indebted she was to this woman, the man from yesterday drove by. Apparently, he had not expected her to be sitting in her car and was looking at the shop when he spotted her. For one brief moment their eyes locked and she knew . . . . *this man is stalking me!*

Panic lasted for a second before she rationalized to herself. *Why am I letting myself get so upset about a man who can't possibly harm me. There's a stakeout somewhere close by and I'm in the middle of a small town where people are good and caring!* With resolve, Susan got out of her car, walked over and unlocked the door of her shop and started turning on all the lights as she walked to the back, determined that she was not going to continue to live in fear. Her shop was going to be completed! Her business was going to prosper! She was going to have a wonderful life! As these thoughts tumbled through her mind, giving her courage, Frank and Mike arrived, followed by the workmen. All was right with the world!

Unknown to Susan, Dominic cursed his bad luck after passing Susan's shop. Then he remembered an adage pounded into his head by his mentor, Sal: *There aint no such thing as bad luck.* You were either stupid or weren't paying attention. Dominic knew what Sal would say about the woman seeing him. He also knew that anything he did would have to be tonight and would have to look like an accident. Maybe el Duce wanted her alive, but dead people told no tales. He needed to make a move now that would give him credibility and at the same time not draw attention to him. *Getz!* The man was an asshole, but he was perfect for Dominic's purpose. Dominic scrolled his phone until the number came up, hit the dial button and waited for the phone to ring.

"Yeh," came the irritating southern twang in his ear. Dominic answered, "Mr. Getz? This is Mr. Smith again. I hate to bother you again but I wondered if you knew of any land available *out* of Martinsville but in the general area, maybe a fifty mile or even a hundred mile radius. There's a substantial referral fee involved if my investors buy." Dominic didn't have to wait long for the reply he anticipated. "Look, Mr. Smith, we don't cotton to you slick outsiders coming in and trying to run our land prices up. So get lost." The resounding *clunk* assured Dominic he had accomplished his purpose. Now all he had to figure out was a plan that would work. *Adios femme fatale* and hello New Orleans!

Susan went over some details with Frank and Mike before resuming cleaning up the mess that accumulated each time from the work being done. Frank had assured Susan that the men were accustomed to cleaning up after themselves, but Susan, unnerved by the many subtle plots unraveling all around her, and not daring to risk offending Frank or the men by pushing them, diplomatically told him, "Your skills are too valuable to waste time using a broom. I'm not doing anything else so why not speed things up by freeing you?" Frank laughed and shook his head, "I have never met a client that had your attitude. Thanks!" Susan suddenly thought of Michelangelo flagellating himself in the Sistine Chapel and immediately thought: *Why on earth did I think of that?*

Dominic drove to the motel where he was staying and checked out, telling Roy, "I'm heading up to Tennessee. I haven't seen my contact, and from what I gather, no one around here seems interested in selling. Know any place to stay outside Chattanooga?" Roy was flabbergasted. The man hadn't said that much to him since he had checked in!

Dominic drove northeast for a couple hours until he came to a small town that suited his purpose. On the outskirts of town he located a general store and parked his car out of sight and went in and bought a pair of jeans, a denim shirt, a ball cap, and a pair of boots. He also bought a rod and reel and a few other supplies, including a lantern and fuel. The man behind the counter totaled everything and remarked, "Looks like you gonna do some fishing." Dominic wanted to say as little as possible, so answered, "Yep," in the vernacular. If he was remembered at all, he wanted to be remembered as the guy from the city who went fishing.

He took his things, drove back toward Martinsville to a motel on the outskirts of a small town, rented a room, asking for a unit off to itself, saying, "I need to get some sleep." He then changed into his new clothes, slipped out the door and walked behind the motel, emerging onto the sidewalk several hundred feet from the motel. He had in his possession a driver license which he had selected from several he kept hidden in the lining of his suitcase. As he walked into town looking for a used car lot, he mentally rehearsed how the person was supposed to sound he was pretending to be. The vogue of the worn look in jeans was to his advantage. He finally found a used car lot and looked for the worst looking car.

The man who approached him had on a suit that needed to go to the cleaners and the look that suggested he was out to take you there. He approached Dominic with, "Howdy stranger. Whatever you want in a good used car I've got. Now the one you're looking at is the cheapest one on the lot. Twenty-five hundred and its yours, or if you can go thirty-five, I've got a nice little four door."

Dominic put on his best southern drawl. "Ah don't need no four door. Ah give you'a thousand fer this'un. The salesman tried to look shocked but secretly was delighted to have such a challenge. "Two thousand and you can take it."

Dominic wanted to slap the salesman up against his crummy piece of junk car but instead said, "Twelve hundred." The salesman broke out in a sweat and his eyes seemed to gleam as he answered, "Eighteen hundred." When Dominic pulled a roll of bills out of his pocket there was a look of triumph on the salesman's face until Dominic countered with, "Mah final offa is Fifteen hundred." The salesman's face took on a momentary abashed look, then he recovered with a smile, a glib "Sold," and a handshake that had been trained by pumping water on a farm. It occurred to Dominic as he drove the shabby car down the road that he would be lucky if the heap hung together until he was finished with it. Maybe hicks weren't as dumb as he thought! Just stealing a car in a large city would be a lot easier. Fifteen hundred would come out of his pocket, not Tony's! *To hell with it!* At least Phase two of his plan was completed.

~ 21 ~

Susan kept the shop debris cleaned up but spent the greater part of her morning arranging the cubbyhole where her desk and file cabinets had been installed. She had accumulated invoices in boxes and was glad to be filing them away. She functioned better when things were in order. Occasionally Frank or Mike would appear and ask a question about some finishing details but assured her the shop would be ready in just a couple of days. The activity had calmed her earlier vexation. She had called Fred Stipe, the insurance man, to discuss taking out a policy on her shop. When she had totaled up her debt for furnishing the shop the amount had shocked her. Everything had cost a lot more than five years ago; it would be a financial disaster for her if the building were to catch on fire. When she heard Frank speak to someone, she looked up expecting to see Stipe and instead found Jay walking in with a deli bag in his hand. "Got time for lunch?" He asked. "Of course," she responded and found a clean cloth and wiped off the desk and chair, then asked, "No lunch date with one of your fellow barristers?" Jay took napkins out and spread them before taking out the sandwiches. Sitting down he said, "I'm afraid you are flattering me and my colleagues. I think we're just plain lawyers. But anyway I prefer to have lunch with you. You're a lot prettier and never so dull as they. Besides, I wanted to see how your shop was coming along."

Susan and Jay had just finished their sandwich when Fred Stipe appeared in the shop. He had brought along papers for Susan to fill out and had an inventory sheet he was jotting things down on. He seemed embarrassed at intruding and almost ran his words together as he said, "Susan, I presume, Fred Stipe. Hello Jay. Good to see you. Sorry, didn't mean to interrupt your lunch," then added, "You two go right ahead while I do a quick inventory." He turned and quickly walked away. Susan and Jay could hear him talking to Frank and Mike.

A few minutes later he came back and shook Susan's and Jay's hand. "Nice set up you've got here Susan. I think the first thing I would suggest is putting in an alarm system. I represent a number of insurance companies and all of them offer a substantial discount if you install a good alarm that also has smoke detection. Makes sense to insurance company and client. Course I have to disclose that my son-in-law owns the local company that would do that, unless you would prefer to bring someone in from Atlanta or Chattanooga." The man was no longer the shy intruder. Now he was an astute businessman ready to do a service for his client. The frailness that seemed to emanate before was now replaced by self confidence. Jay spoke up quietly, "I think Susan would be delighted to have Joe install a system. Right Susan?" Susan was a little surprised at Jay making a decision for her but none the less answered, "Great." Fred lost no time getting on his cell phone. He walked off a little distance from the couple then turned and asked Susan, "Would this afternoon be convenient for you? He can be finished by seven." "Of course," Susan agreed.

When Fred left, Jay explained. "Fred is the salt of the earth and Joe is very dependable. Most people would not bother to disclose the connection. You'll get a good job at a reasonable price and with the suspicion surrounding Getz, you don't want to take a chance. There's not such a demand for alarm systems around here so Joe's company works in the surrounding towns."

For the first time since her father died, Susan felt both completely secure while maintaining her independence. Both Jay and Julia were assertive by nature; however, Susan never felt coerced or manipulated—just taken care of in the way that her dad had taken care of her: Offering solutions but never forcing those solutions on her. *Life is good!*

After Jay left, Susan decided to run to the store and pick up her ingredients for the canapés for Mildred Brice's reception. She told Frank and Mike if Joe came to tell him to go ahead and start the job. Susan had been so preoccupied with getting her shop ready and *other* things, she didn't realize how much she missed her work. The thoughts of throwing herself into this reception made her feel revitalized. She was back within the hour and carried in several large boxes, stepping over electric cords as the additional workmen did their job. The large commercial refrigerators had been plugged in. The cold hit her face as she opened the door. The large expanse of space was a welcome sight and she was reminded of Julia's refrigerator and the problems she would have faced if these hadn't come in. Everything was ready except the large stoves that had been delivered just minutes ago. Frank and Mike were connecting them while a man from the gas company inspected the outlets. Susan had thought she could work here today but with the additional activity it would be impossible.

Making a decision, she approached the man she assumed was Joe. “Excuse me. Are you Joe?” A young man of about medium height, with freckles, and a grin that showed a mouthful of crooked but healthy looking teeth, stood up, wiped his hands on a towel hanging out of his jeans pocket and extended his hand, “Yes ma'am, you must be Ms. Sullivan. Nice to meet you.” “How long will you be working here today?” Susan asked. “We'll be here til seven thirty probably. Is that gonna be a problem?” He softly responded. Susan understood Jay's endorsement of this man. His words came out like molasses—warm and flowing. His eyes were blue and totally without guile. Susan answered him with gratitude, “Not at all, in fact I'm so pleased you were able to jump into the job so quickly. Thanks. I'll be working over at the Martin house if you need me for anything, but I'll be back before you finish. In fact I'm glad I won't have to come back to a dark shop.” Joe beamed another grin at Susan and said, “You go right ahead and do what you have to do. Like I say, we'll probably be here til seven thirty or after.”

Susan pulled out some of the large trays that arrived two days ago and starting taking them to her car. She needed the van but until the local body shop rigged it with the tray racks that were on order, her car would have to do. What had seemed like an inconvenience now loomed larger and the pressure of her efforts being fragmented was taking its toll on both her energy and nerves. After several trips to her car, one of the men asked her, “Ma'am, do you need some help?” Her emphatic “Yes!” was due to gratitude but sounded so explosive she thought she had scared him. Her additional, “Thank you, thank you so much,” was further softened with a smile, and with his help, Susan's things were soon loaded. As she drove back to the Martin house, she was grateful that after today she would not be working in two locations.

Julia arrived at four fifteen from the library finding Susan still chopping. Still everything had to be mixed before making the canapés. Precious minutes were lost in transporting everything. Susan's earlier enthusiasm had been dampened and was replaced by a frantic desire to get back to the shop before Joe left. The need to finish the canapés was secondary to the fear of returning to the empty shop. She had always worked with deadlines and pressure but never fear that brought on a sense of panic. Julia insisted on helping, but Susan couldn't shake the feeling of dread. She said very little as they worked. Julia, sensing something was wrong, asked, "You seem distracted. Is there anything you need to talk about?"

As much regard as Susan felt for Julia, she was unable to discuss her fears with her, so she responded by answering her with a question totally from out of nowhere, "Julia, are you going to do the food for Jay's and my wedding reception?"

Julia, mistaking Susan's reason for asking this, probed, "Is there something you have in mind?" Susan's ploy had backfired. *Now Julia thought she didn't want her help!* Before Susan could reply, Julia, unperturbed went on, "Of course dear, you two can decide what you want and if you have a special recipe, just let me know."

Susan, with all the help from Julia, soon saw the time gap closing. Still, She knew Julia would want to go to the hospital and visit Velma and Henry and she didn't need any extra worry. Trying to quell her unreasonable anxiety and talk about something that was of interest to Julia, Susan blurted out the first thing she could think of to pull Julia's attention away from anything depressive. "Julia, what should we name our first boy?"

The question was so completely *not* Susan that Julia looked up at her in surprise. "Well dear, I think you and Jay need to decide that." Julia thought for a moment, then added, "But perhaps you might think about paying homage to your father and Jay's father by combining a name from each. I believe I remember your dad's name was James Conner Sullivan and Jay's father was John Randolph Martin. You could name a boy James Randolph Martin or John Conner Martin. What do you think dear, does either name appeal to you?"

Both women were so engrossed in their topic that neither heard Jay come in and were startled when he asked, "I like the sound of both. Now what are we going to name the other six?"

Susan's concentration had been intent on getting the canapés finished so that Jay's appearance took her by surprise. Julia spoke up, "Jay dear, I think you need to let Susan know when you're kidding. She may take you seriously."

Jay walked over to Susan, put his arms around her and kissed her on the cheek. "What do you say Susan? We both want children, but how many?"

Susan was not to be outdone. She looked at Jay and answered, "Probably four or five. Two or three boys and two girls."

Jay pondered her answer for a moment then asked, "Why not three girls and two boys or four boys and one girl?"

Susan knew at once that Jay was testing her to see if she had answered in a frivolous way. With confidence she confronted his challenge. "I don't think it would be fair to have four boys and one girl. The boys would be constantly complaining that the girl was spoiled and received preferential treatment. And they would probably be right! Besides, she would be lonely. Three boys can get along better than three girls. Girls can be petty sometimes and play odd man out. So there you are."

Jay just stood looking at Susan as Julia remarked, "Susan, I knew you were smart but now I think you're also wise."

Jay looked at his mother then at Susan before remarking, "If I didn't appreciate good food so much I would say you are wasting your talent on catering and should become a trial lawyer. Julia's right. I hope all five of our children take after you. Now how about a drink to that?"

Susan was acutely aware that time was slipping away. The canapés had to be finished and taken to the shop to chill. She protested, "I can't. I have to get all the canapés to the shop before Joe leaves!"

"Why?" Jay queried.

Susan was stuck. She hated to involve Jay after he had worked all day. "Susan," he said patiently, guessing her motive, "If we're going to have five children, we are going to have pull together. And that includes having the pleasure of a glass of wine in the evening. I'll help you transport the food to the shop later. Right now, let's have a glass of wine."

Julia spoke up, "There's cold chicken salad and Brie with apple crisps for later. I need to run over to the hospital and see about Velma and Henry after we have our wine." Susan knew Jay and Julia would not take no for an answer, so gracefully accepted their help, knowing such help would be perpetuated in the future, allowing her to have a career and five children without neglecting anyone. As she followed Julia and Jay to the porch, she was thinking: *James Randolph Martin, John Conner Martin, Sullivan Prescott Martin, Julia Tiffany Martin, and Susan Alexandria Martin. Wow!*

~ 22 ~

Ralph Getz was perturbed. There were things going on he couldn't quite understand but felt they might relate to his *questionable* activities. He had caught sight of Jerry Moore lurking around the building on Beech street. Then finding Susan snooping around in the other side of the building had unnerved him. *Thank God I had scrubbed up that blood. Now all I have to worry about is getting that well filled up.*

The well. Ralph thought about Vera. He probably hadn't come as close to causing permanent damage to her as he did last night. It had started after he passed near *that* well on his way home yesterday afternoon. He'd noticed the buzzard's circling. Vera had told him Bart had filled the old well. When he questioned her he found out she'd thought he meant the old well on her daddy's place. He then hit her. And when she whined he just kept hitting her. After he calmed down he told her if Julia Martin came out to see her she was to say she fell down the stairs in the basement. Stupid woman. He thought of the life he might've had if he'd married someone with a little get up and go. He and Vera had grown up together on adjacent farms. Her old man was more of a worker than his dad and had more land. Vera's mom died when she was twelve and that's when he and she started their fling in her old man's hayloft. That went on for a long time before the old man caught them and forced Ralph to marry his *ruined* daughter.

Since Vera had inherited the farm after the old man died, his marriage was a little more tolerable. They'd never had children, so at least there were no added problems. But what seemed good to a young man just starting to feel his oats didn't hold his interest once he was married. While the old man was alive, Ralph had to go out of the area to find new women to satisfy his desire for variety. It wouldn't do to lose the land by Vera divorcing him.

Ralph loaded three bags of lime on the back of his truck and drove to the well. He dragged the bags over the edge of the well and emptied them, figuring it would stop the stench and discourage the buzzards. Bart could fill in the well later. Back in his truck he drove along thinking of the deputy hovering around his place in town. The best way to cover his ass was to dismantle the machine and take it out to the old barn on Vera's dad's place. It suddenly occurred to him that he still thought of the place as belonging to the old man, even after he'd talked Vera into transferring it to his name. He'd told her it would make the land more attractive to a land investor if the two tracts of land were combined.

Ralph spent half his time repairing the old outbuildings on the two farms. There was always something to tear down and rebuild. He drove out to the old barn that Vera's daddy had built. You had to hand it to the old man. When he built a barn it was meant to last. It took Ralph a couple of hours to examine and make a few changes to the barn. The windows were nailed shut to prevent curious folks from entering that way. Then he put locks on the front and back doors. By the time he'd swept the trash out that had accumulated over the years, it was noon. He still needed to repair some parts of the roof that had shone signs of leaking. He wasn't in a hurry. The machine could be broken down in a couple hours. He'd do that at supper time while everyone was occupied; then load it in his truck after dark when he'd be least likely to be seen. Besides it was Friday. Baseball game tonight.

As Ralph rode back to his house he was a satisfied man. Since Susan had rented the place next door to his operation, he'd felt cramped. The people up in Tennessee had placed an order that he hadn't been able to fill because of the activity created by her and the law. Ralph had a generator that would run the machine and there was no one to see or hear out in the country. Walking into the kitchen where Vera was cooking his lunch, he felt a kind of pity for her. Apparently he had broken her nose. It spread all over her face and connected her eyes and mouth into sort of a dough-like appearance. He ate quickly, feeling a revulsion when she faced him.

Ralph spent the rest of the afternoon patching the roof of the barn and moving the generator to supply the electricity. Going back to the house, he was hoping Vera would be lying down so he wouldn't have to look at her. She usually wasn't a bad looking woman. However, living with an abusive husband had taken its toll on her. Of course Ralph wasn't one to accept that responsibility. Like most abusers, he thought *if she'd just do the right thing.* The tell tale sign in her eyes that usually looked downward in a face old before its time were classic signs of abuse. Ralph had just a shred of conscience left to feel slightly guilty; but even that made him angry with Vera. He went into the house, took a quick shower and left for town without seeing her. Good. *She must never know the activities that would be taking place in her daddy's old barn!*

Meanwhile, headed to the same destination, Dominic drove the junker into Martinsville before sundown. He was fine tuning his plans for the evening in his mind when he spotted a banner attached to utility poles and draped high across the street reading: BASEBALL ~ MARTINSVILLE vs. STILLWELL, FRIDAY NIGHT 7:30

When he drove by Susan's shop he saw the workmen still busy and didn't wonder why there was no vehicle parked out front. Frank and Mike, now gone, had taken up the parking spaces earlier in the day so that Joe had parked his van emblazoned with STEWART'S LOCK & ALARM SYSTEMS in the back of the building.

Dominic figured the men probably wouldn't be working too much longer, so he drove out to a local bar and grill where he settled down to food and drink He had constructed his *surprise* for Susan before he left the motel last night. His plan was to connect this to the oven in the shop. He could be in and out of her shop in fifteen minutes. When she lighted the stove the next day, her *surprise* would be her last. Boom! And the beauty of the plan was he'd be miles away in Atlanta or maybe even landing at the airport in New Orleans. The thought of finally ending this job almost brought a smile to Dominic's face, but smiling was something he'd left behind in a childhood filled with violence.

As he sat waiting for dark to make his move, across town Ralph Getz drove around to the back of his building and parked his truck, backing it in so he could load up without drawing any attention from the men working next door. He got out and took his tool box inside. Once inside he locked his door and went to the room where the machinery was located. As he passed the spot where the stain was still partially visible in spite of his scrubbing, he made a mental note to bring a bottle of Clorox from home.

If the law were to test that spot, it might be hard to explain how he got so much blood on the floor!

Next door, Jay and Susan brought the canapés before Joe had finished installing the alarm system. The two men working with Joe were eating hamburgers, apparently too hungry to wait. Joe, however, was hard at work. He stopped long enough to say hello to Jay and Susan before resuming his work with, "Ms. Susan, we'll be finished in another thirty minutes. The guys had to stop and eat. Said their backbones were sticking into their rib cage!"

"Don't worry Joe. We'll hang around for awhile," Susan replied.

"We'll be back in about twenty minutes Joe," Jay added.

Susan looked at Jay wondering what he was up to. She took his hand and pulled him over where the men couldn't hear, "Jay, when I see that eyebrow of yours it sets off my own personal alarm. What's up?"

"We're taking a little ride. We'll be back in time to lock up."

With that he took Susan's arm and guided her out to his car where he opened the door for her, then went around and hopped into the driver's seat. They drove to the spot where he had taken her as a stranger a few weeks before. He parked the car and sat there a moment looking out on the same scene where he had talked about his ancestors, then he turned to her and said, "When I brought you up here the first time, I just wanted to sit here until I had the nerve to kiss you. I talked about my family legacy. I'm proud of them and wanted you to see what I had to live up to. When I looked at you it occurred to me that you had that same kind of pride. There was an aura about you that stopped me. I didn't want to ruin my chances with you."

Jay reached over and pulled Susan to his side and kissed her. They sat for a few minutes not saying a word, just looking out on the landmarks that were dear to Jay's heart and soon would be equally endearing to Susan, then they drove back to the shop where Joe and his men were picking up their tools to leave.

"Wanna try the system out and see how it sounds?" Joe asked.

Susan was a little shy of making a commotion that might attract people. "Mind if I pass on that, Joe?" Susan answered. Jay looked at his watch. Seven twenty-five.

He told Susan, "They're starting the ball game in five minutes. There'll be so much yelling by the crowd, no one's going to pay attention to the alarm. Joe can cut it off in seconds. Try it."

Susan just nodded her head for Joe to trigger it. The sound was shocking even though she was prepared. Joe quickly turned it off saying to her, "Watch."

“What did you do?” She asked.

“There’s a tiny little release lever right here that you push. No one else will know about it except you. You have exactly five minutes after the lever is pushed to enter your secret code. If you don’t enter the code, the alarm will not sound here again but will at our central station where the police will be notified. That way if someone were to force you to stop the alarm you could do it and then after five minutes someone would come to your aid.” Joe was obviously proud of his system.

Joe left, leaving Jay and Susan to lock up and set the alarm. After doing so they headed home. Tomorrow was going to be a busy day. Susan had to arrive at the shop by seven, finish and deliver the food, supervise serving until the reception was over, then clean up. Home by twelve midnight was her goal. But that was tomorrow. Right now her goal was a hot bath and eight solid hours of sleep.

When they walked into the foyer, Julia insisted the two sit down to the chicken salad and brie while she gave the latest news on Velma and Henry. When finished, Susan started to collect the dishes; Julia stopped her and insisted she retire. Susan was too tired to protest as Jay escorted her down the hall and kissed her goodnight outside their rooms. Tomorrow was her debut as the *chef de cuisine.*

~ 23 ~

As Dominic drove down the main street in Martinsville, the street lights had just come on. Susan's shop was dark except for a small light shining faintly through an inner door. *Good. Enough light to see by but dark enough to conceal.* He had considered parking the old car under the tree in the church yard but spotted the glow of a cigarette. Probably some kid sneaking a smoke. He drove around until he found a spot where the car would be quick to get to but unlikely to attract attention, got out and walked to the back of the shop, spotting Ralph Getz's truck. *Shit!* Dominic hesitated a minute, mulling over his options, slipped a small jimmy into the side of the lock, then realized it was a dead bolt. The adjacent door sounded as the deadbolt was turned. Dominic moved behind the door as Ralph Getz struggled out with the first of the dismantled machinery. As the door closed behind him, he shoved the load onto the back of the truck. Suddenly aware of someone's presence, he turned and faced Dominic seconds before the jimmy connected. Instead of hitting the back of his head, Dominic caught Ralph across the temple causing him to fall forward almost knocking Dominic's feet out from under him. Dominic grabbed Ralph's shirt and eased him to the ground, then turned him over revealing his identity. Searching quickly, he found the keys in Ralph's pocket and tried each one on the door lock to Susan's shop. When the bolt turned he imagined himself already in the plane to New Orleans with money in his pocket. As he stepped over the threshold the alarm sounded—a sound he had heard so many times in his life but simply hadn't anticipated now. It didn't compute in his brain. A little hick town was not supposed to have alarm systems! Seconds passed before realizing his dilemma, then he bolted. He skirted the building behind him and found an alley, and, forcing himself to walk at a normal pace, worked his way back to the junker, He got in, started it and drove in the opposite direction until he was in the outskirts of town, passing a patrol car with its siren screaming full blast heading back to town. His first inclination was to keep going. *To hell with the whole thing!* But the further he drove, the more sure he was that he would live to regret it. *If he lived!* The fear of getting caught in Martinsville was nothing compared to the fear of facing the Vascolas. He turned around at the next cross road and headed back to Martinsville.

Larry Pittman had just finished his run to the outskirts of town when he got the call from the night dispatcher at headquarters. He recognized the address as Ralph Getz's building. "Damn," he said out loud. "I watched that place a week and as soon as I go back to patrolling, something happens!" The dispatcher, apparently not cut off, blasted over the speaker, "Well just get your ass over there Larry and quit the bitching!" Larry was trying to decide whether or not to turn on his siren when a car started across an intersection in front of him. He slammed on brakes and hit the siren simultaneously. The car he narrowly missed lost control for a second and went up on the sidewalk before the driver was able to stop. Larry kept going and pulled in front of Getz's building with a screech of his tires. There were already a couple of officers in the back of the building leaning over Ralph, and Larry could see an ambulance coming. He decided to escort the ambulance to the hospital. Considering his close call down the road, there was a safety factor to be considered.

After Ralph was loaded into the ambulance, Larry turned on his siren and drove down main street toward the hospital. He had no reason to hurry. The medic had checked Ralph and said his vital signs were good. *This was the most exciting thing that had ever happened to Larry in his short career and he wanted to prolong it!*

A relay was started when the police chief was called at home. He in turn called Jay who awakened Susan and Julia. It was decided that Julia would ride out with an officer in a police car to the Getz farm to pick up Vera and bring her to the hospital. The woman was too fragile emotionally to go it alone. Jay and Susan went on to the shop to see if anything had been disturbed. They were totally perplexed as to why anyone would want to break into her shop. No one had paid the slightest bit of attention to the box on the back of Ralph's truck. They had been wanting to get into Ralph's side of the building for weeks and finally had the authority to do so tonight. Once inside Ralph's side of the building they found nothing but boxes of completely dismantled equipment that was not suspicious because it was packed with a bunch of junk. It was Jay who finally offered the possible explanation for the assault on Ralph when he examined the box on the truck. His reasoning was that the adversary had gone into the wrong door after he had attacked Ralph, setting off the alarm. The police chief arrived about the time Jay made the discovery of the credit card blanks.

"Evening, Mac, did we get you away from the game?"

"No Jay, I can't sit that long in one spot anymore. What's Ralph been up to?"

"Looks like he finally hit the big time—credit card forging."

"The stupid S.O.B. He's already got more money than anyone in the county."

Chief Wallace walked into the door of Ralph Getz's side of the building and immediately noticed the remainder of a stain in front of the door leading to the rest of the boxes. "Bert," he called out in what might be described as a subdued bellow.

Bert Cross was second in command and Chief Wallace's prized officer. He had been trained in forensics in D.C. before he finally bailed out and came back home to a *kinder, gentler* environment. Bert walked over to the spot Wallace was pointing and whistled. "Doesn't look good, Chief. Let me go get my equipment and I'll get right onto it." The chief turned to Jay and asked, "When's the last time Julia went out to see Vera?" Jay saw what was on Mac's mind and assured him, "I don't think it's Vera's blood. Larry took Julia out to her home to pick her up and I've heard from Julia. They're at the hospital with Ralph."

There was a look that Mac had seen on Jay's face before. He knew Jay was probably the smartest lawyer around and it was like watching a computer monitor before it spit out the answers. "Something you need to tell me Jay?"

"No. No," he replied. But Mac had a feeling Jay was holding back something.

Since credit card forgery was both a GBI and an FBI matter, Chief Mac Wallace left to go back to his office and call personally. He had an ulterior motive in wanting Bert to do his forensic investigation before they were inundated with the *big brothers* of law enforcement. *They* had such a way of making you feel you were a dumb hick with hay sticking out of your ears. Besides, he wanted to see if he could ferret out whatever secret was residing in Jay Martin's mind. Meanwhile, he would have Larry and Bert go over everything in the computer found in Ralph's building. This would be a busy day indeed

His friend with the State Troopers had set up road blocks in all the main roads leading out of Martinsville, ostensibly to check that people were using current driver's license. He had an hour or two at the most before he had to call on the big guns, and he wanted to give every law officer in the county the opportunity to practice his skills before being cast aside. *They don't understand how frustrating it can get to never get to practice those skills. The trouble with life is—its usually feast or famine. Not just in law enforcement but in every damned thing!*

Across the street in the shadow of the tree, Dominic watched and tried to plan his next move. Now, after all his well-laid plans, he had an eye witness. He felt the burden of complications pulling him into some invisible trap from which there was no way out.

Dominic waited within the shelter of the tree for the greater part of an hour but still the police hung around the site. Dominic's patience had worn thin and he was about to leave when he recognized Jay getting into his car. Dominic quickly retreated through the back of the church lot to where he had hidden his car behind a fence. By the time he started the old car, Jay had driven past and only his tail lights were visible in the distance. Dominic lagged behind the car, knowing anything out of the ordinary would cause suspicion. When Jay pulled into the driveway of his home, Dominic drove past, going around the block, seeking an obscure place to park his car. There was a lane behind the large houses, a throw-back to the days when servants and delivery people weren't allowed in the front door. Dominic turned off his lights and carefully eased the old car down the lane until he was behind the Martin home. There he found a perfect place to conceal his car—beside a gardening shed. He looked around to see if any lights came on in response to his entrance—nothing. He debated about staying in the car in case he had to leave quickly, but the car would never outrun anything on the road, so he decided to investigate the property and either find Susan or an entry for later. This was his last chance.

He carefully opened the door of the car and was slipping out when he was suddenly blinded by a light. It took several seconds before his eyes recovered from the shock. He stood frozen, watching as Jay walked across the back yard to the adjoining property, unlock the back door, and enter the neighbor's home. Dominic stood, half in, half out of the car, afraid to move. If he ran, the police would have him in minutes. If he stayed, his car would be seen when Jay came out. He stayed in this awkward position for several minutes before he decided to take a chance and start the motor of the car. Just before he turned the starter, the lights on the back of the house went off! *Damn motion sensor lights.* He sucked in his breath and waited for Jay to come out of the house. Five minutes later, Jay stepped out of the back door and the neighbor's sensor lights came back on. Jay stood with his back to Dominic and locked the door, turned and started back across the yard to his own back door. He was carrying a bundle and never looked in the direction of the gardening shed. When the sensor lights came on as Jay approached his own back door, the side of the gardening shed was out of his line of vision.

Dominic sat very still cursing his bad luck and looking at his watch. The lights went off after five minutes unless there was motion. It suddenly dawned on him that he had been spared the probability of either getting caught or shot. Now he knew where the sensor lights were, how they were timed, and how far their light extended. This knowledge made him again bold. He slipped out of the car, circumvented the area that would trigger the lights, and keeping close to the side of house, watched as Jay got back into his car and pulled out of the driveway.

The next thing he needed to find out was whether the Martin home had an alarm system. He carefully worked his way around the house looking for a meter. Old houses usually had outside meters. Finally locating it, he pulled the main switch and then looked for the easiest way of gaining entry. Within ten minutes he was inside the house and located Susan's bedroom where he unlocked the window on the front and on the side. He wanted a choice. Within fifteen minutes of entry, he was back outside flipping the main switch back on before leaving when he remembered seeing digital clocks!

He had seen no sign of an alarm system, but he would have to chance it. Without flipping the main switch again, he went back inside, and going from room to room he changed the clocks. He was about to leave when he remembered the coffee maker, reset it, slipped out again, and made it to the back of the gardening shed when a car pulled into the driveway. His hands were sweaty, and his heart was racing wildly. Damn! Never again would he take on a job in a small town! There was no where to go. No where to hide. People knew you were a stranger and watched you like a hawk, and he *still* had the job to do. He eased himself into the car and settled down for a long wait.

~ 24 ~

Julia was particularly robust for a lady in her sixties; however, even the more hearty members of what is considered *the elderly* need about eight hours rest. Upon hearing of Ralph's hospitalization, Julia thought of the impact this news would have on his wife, so volunteered to go out to the Getz farm to console and support her. Julia had no idea what Ralph had done to the poor woman the day before and upon seeing her, she realized what had occurred. Any sympathy Julia had mustered up for Ralph quickly disintegrated. She accompanied Vera to the hospital in the police car and insisted that she be admitted to the hospital as well. While Ralph had a mild concussion and a wound that required ten stitches and bed rest for twenty-four hours, Vera's visit would entail x-rays, various tests, a nose reconstruction, and a thorough exam by a clinical psychologist. She was terrified of Ralph, but Julia calmed her fears by promising her she would be taken by ambulance to Atlanta, and Ralph would not be allowed to see her.

Julia left the hospital after the sedative given to Vera took effect. She'd sat by the woman's bedside holding her hand as though she were a frightened child, rather than chronologically, Julia's age. At moments like this, Julia was keenly aware that while we may all be equal in the sight of God, truly—we are not equal!

When Julia had left to go out to Vera's, she assured Jay she would call him when she was ready to go home. As it turned out she called a taxi. The crisp air was inspiring as she walked to the cab wishing she were ten years younger so she could walk home. *That* would expend some of the agitation she now felt pulsing in her body causing what she imagined to be some sort of malignant toxins. *Ralph Getz had gone too far for the last time!* Slipping out of the cab after paying her fare, she was met in the foyer by a distraught Susan and a perplexed Jay who stood there shaking his head asking, "Why didn't you call us?" As if in answer to his own question a smile crossed Jay's face before he spoke. "Dear Julia, one of these days you are going to accept my help?"

Julia let out a merry little laugh before asking, "Are you making a statement or asking a question?"

Susan suddenly understood the dynamics involved in the scene that had unfolded between mother and son. Julia was going to be independent as long as she had a breath left in her. Jay, on the other hand, while accepting of her need to be independent, knew she had never encountered violence that could remotely involve her until now. *Ralph could have died!*. In fact, where had the blood come from on the floor in Ralph's building? Someone sinister had penetrated the sanctity of Martinsville.

Realizing she had worried both Susan and Jay, Julia now wanted to end the discussion and go to bed. Her "Sorry dears, ... night," while contrite, put an end to further comments! Jay turned to watch his mother retreat to her bedroom and felt Susan's arm slip around his waist as she asked, "Are you sure you want five children? They may not be any easier to handle than Julia."

"But we can spank them," Jay remarked with resolve. "Now to bed with you, woman! You were supposed to get eight hours sleep and I can only suppose you'll do some tossing and turning like the rest of us." With that statement, he kissed Susan and the two went to their separate room. After Susan turned on her bedroom light and was slipping off her blouse, a strange feeling gave her a chill. The thought *I'm just tired* answered the *what's wrong with me.* Looking around the room, she spotted what had jangled her nerves. One of her curtains was pulled ever so slightly awry. Going over to straighten it, she wondered if Julia had the woman who helped around the house occasionally in for a quick spruce-up. What with Susan's reception tomorrow and trying to tend to Velma and Henry's affairs, it made sense. Satisfying herself that this was the case, she dismissed it from her mind and finished dressing for bed. Settling into her covers, she heard the song in her mind, *Tomorrow, tomorrow, it's only a day away.* Then she drifted off into a deep sleep.

In her dream, Susan was back in the cave-like passage, deep in the Mayan pyramid in Mexico with her father. Claustrophobia had always been an issue with her, but she had been determined to go with her father to see the *Kings Room,* located inside the center of the pyramid. Within twenty feet after entering the passageway, there was a posted warning that if you wanted to turn back you had to do so at that point. She went ahead relentlessly but was hyperventilating by the time she got out. In her dream something was wrong. She wasn't hyperventilating. Instead, something was hurting her neck and there was a terrible weight on her chest. She felt herself spinning around as if she had fallen into an abyss. There was a crash and then a sudden burst of light. When she regained consciousness, Jay was on the floor holding her, telling her to breathe. Julia was holding the phone with one hand and a pistol with the other, apparently talking to—who? Nothing made sense. She had been in the pyramid with her father. Reality took hold. She fought to sit up while Jay kept saying, "It's okay, it's okay. Just take some deep breaths." Jay, sensing her need to sit up, lifted her so that she sat on the bed. He sat next to her with his arm around her giving support. He said nothing, just let her take in the scene: her open window, the broken lamp on the floor, and beside the lamp—a strange—no, not strange man. It was the man who had asked about land several days ago in her shop. Sirens sounded. A shudder ran through her body. Jay enquired,. "Who is he?"

"He's the man I told you about the other day, asking if the shop was for sale."

"Julia, let me have the gun and go let the police in."

Dominic had lain very quietly, faking unconsciousness and waiting for the right moment to act when he heard the siren. As Julia leaned over to hand the gun to Jay, Dominic caught her ankle with a backward sweep of his elbow, knocking her backward. Jay grabbed the gun, pushed Susan behind him, shielding her. Julia, sprawled next to Dominic, tried to get up but he brought his arm around her neck. Larry Pitman burst into the room, immediately sized up the situation. Bounding across the room, he brought his fist down the side of Dominic's head, tearing the ear and catching the edge of the eyelid as the little edges of his Police Academy ring caught on the tender flesh. This time Dominic didn't feign anything—he was out cold. Julia disentangled herself and stood up, rubbing her ankle. Looking down on Dominic she remarked, "So that's what they mean by cold cocking someone. Nicely done, Larry!" She then turned to Susan and softly asked, "How are you doing dear?" Susan didn't, couldn't say a word. She pushed herself up off the bed and aided by Jay, hugged Julia and asked, "Is there anything you're afraid of?"

"Of course," Julia answered, "Not having grandchildren and not being useful!"

By three o'clock A.M. Susan was back in bed and fell asleep with the help of a sedative and Jay rubbing her back. Dr. James had come and prescribed a sedative for Susan and a cold pack for Julia's ankle. When he had attended both the ladies, he asked Jay, "Well, how about you, need anything?" Jay thought carefully before answering, "Yes, about three fingers of Scotch." Then he thanked the doctor and saw him to the door. Later, after everyone had gone and Susan was asleep, he walked through each room in the house, checking every lock on doors and windows, then sat in the large chair that had once been his fathers favorite chair and thought about the events of the evening. Sleep was out of the question, or so he thought.

When he awakened, Susan was gently shaking his shoulder. "Jay, Jay—go to bed." One eye viewed her through thick black lashes. The other eye finally opened before he acknowledged her presence. "Don't you want some help?' he asked. Susan laughed before she answered, "That horrible man is in jail. Ralph is under arrest at the hospital and I have three people waiting for instructions at the shop. If you can't go back to sleep, at least keep an eye on Julia and make her stay off that ankle." She then leaned over and kissed Jay on the top of his head before leaving. Jay noticed she had a silk scarf loosely tied around her neck, concealing the marks made by her encounter with Dominic last night. Jay had raised his voice saying, "Give me something *feasible* to do," when he heard the front door slam.

He sat quietly thinking over the events of the previous evening. The song *Maria* from the musical *The Sound of Music* went through his mind. He now had two such women to contend with. *Keep Julia off her ankle? No way!* As if to emphasize his point, the sound of breakfast preparation came from the kitchen. It was going to be a long day.

During the course of the morning, Susan made two trips to pick up supplies while her crew worked in the shop. So far the simple chores were being accomplished without a hitch. By noon Susan had the things to be chilled in the large refrigerators and still managed to prepare a quick and tasty lunch for the team. At the risk of piquing everyone's curiosity, she finally removed the scarf revealing her neck. The bruises and cuts left from the wire garrote were stinging. If anyone wondered, they were discretely silent. By five o'clock the first of the canapés were baking in the ovens and Susan had decorated and prepared the tables at the country club for the food. Everything had to be timed and executed in the proper order for best results and Susan was a perfectionist. The last of the food had come out of the ovens and had been carried in warmers to its destination. The reception was to start at seven but six thirty was the deadline for readiness. The punch sparkled with iridescent splendor. The bottles of champagne were chilled and the glasses arranged in a pyramid that glowed like an inverted chandelier, one of Susan's signature creations. When Julia and Jay made their appearance, they looked refreshed and clear-eyed. Julia's ankle seemed fine, and Susan could only guess she was full of Ibuprofen. They left Susan alone to weld her magic over the food while they welded their social magic over the crowd. One of the chores Susan had to keep pushing was getting her workers to constantly replace the trays with fresh food so there was always a pristine and bountiful look to the tables. Five waiters had been employed to circulate among the guests, replenishing drinks and removing all abandoned food and drink.

A little before ten o'clock over half of the crowd had left, leaving the usual hangers-on to run their course. Susan had sent one of the crew back to the shop to load up the huge dish washer. She had just made her final round of the tables when an unexpected arm went around her waist. The memory of last night had left her feeling a little apprehensive. She stiffened, then relaxed as Jay's voice whispered in her ear, "Lovely lady, this club has never seen nor tasted the likes of the banquet you just served. I'm quoting people. See you at the shop after I take Julia home." He gave her a wink before leaving.

~ 25 ~

At eleven thirty Susan and Jay were at her shop removing the second load of dishes from the huge dish washer when Mac Wallace came by. He wanted to ask Susan a few questions about the prisoner such as: Did she know him? Had she any idea why he wanted to kill her? Susan had no idea where this questioning was leading but was extremely grateful she was not sitting in a room at the station house under strong lights.

"I first saw the man when he came in the shop a few days ago. But he certainly wasn't dressed in jeans. He said he was looking for land for developers, I believe, and he had on a business suit and dark glasses. Later, I'm sure it was him parked across the street under that large oak. The idea seemed ridiculous but I felt he was spying on me and told Jay about it when I got home."

The chief looked over at Jay to collaborate her story. Jay nodded in agreement then said, "I think you need to talk to someone in Atlanta at FBI headquarters Mac. Call Bruce Nesmith and he'll probably be able to connect this man to the Vascolas in West Palm Beach. They're part of a cartel in Florida under investigation."

The police chief directed his next question to Susan.

"So Ms. Sullivan, what was your connection to this cartel?"

Jay chose to ignore the chief's intention and continued to answer for Susan.

"Susan met the Vascolas through her catering service in West Palm Beach. The younger Vascola is a thug and a bully. He seems to think Susan knows something that would get them convicted, probably of money laundering. From what happened the other night, we assume he has a contract out on her. She's talked to the Feds in Atlanta and the DA knows all about it. Talk to him."

Jay's words were quietly spoken but Mac looked at him and knew—end of discussion. He left looking stone-faced.

Susan and Jay managed to put everything in order at the shop and said goodnight outside their bedroom doors before midnight. The rigors of the previous day's events left them exhausted, so sleep came quickly. Sunday morning greeted them with the smell of hot coffee and home baked croissants. Susan slipped on her robe and went out to the kitchen where Julia was reading the paper and eating a croissant with peach preserves.

"Surely you didn't bake these from scratch this morning?"

"No, dear. They were frozen. I put them out last night to thaw."

Susan seemed to collapse into the chair next to Julia and declared in a low voice, "You're too perfect, Julia. How can I ever come up to your standard?" Julia looked surprised, then her face softened. "Susan, you're a fantastic woman. Last night's reception was beyond excellent. You did all of that after almost getting killed. I think you need to have a glass of milk and a croissant and go back to bed. You're tired."

Julia got up and poured a glass of milk for Susan who just sat and shook her head and tried to ignore a tear that had started to run down her check. She sipped the milk and reflected on her tendency lately to burst into tears and realized what bothered her was not being in control! For years she had forced herself to be strong, to set goals and to accomplish them while establishing a barrier that ignored her needs as a female. Sexuality was about being a female and sex was only part of that. When Jay penetrated that barrier, she wasn't prepared for the sense of vulnerability she now felt. Trying to shake off the feelings now bombarding her, she told Julia, "I've been so busy feeling sorry for myself I haven't even asked about your ankle."

Julia reached over and gently patted Susan on the hand. "Prescott women are tough as nails. That man should be glad that Jay ended up with the gun. If I'd had that gun in my hand when he knocked me down I would have shot him."

The image of this gentle and righteous woman shooting anyone suddenly struck Susan as ludicrous. She started a small giggle that slowly erupted into laughing. Julia tipped her head and widened her eyes at Susan until the laughing subsided.

"Susan," she said emphatically, "I do not allow people to abuse me or my love ones." Susan decided she'd better finish her milk and croissant and go back to bed. On the way back to her bedroom, she met Jay in the hall dressed in a suit. Before she could say anything he took her by the shoulders, kissed her on the cheek and told her, "I have usher duty at church today. Julia insists on going to church and later to the hospital, and you need to go back to bed. See you at lunch." He turned and was gone before Susan could reply. Opening her bedroom door, the window where the man had entered caught her eye. Her hand went to the laceration around her neck and a shudder that hit a five on the Richter scale rippled through her body. Even though it was broad daylight and people passed on their way to church, she checked her windows before she laid down. She was thinking before she fell asleep *I'll rest for just a little.*

When she awakened, groggy with sleep, she *felt* rather then heard someone in the room. Expecting to see Jay, she tucked her shoulder in to roll over as something slammed against the back of her head. When she awakened again, she had something stuffed in her mouth and a cover of some kind over her head. Her arms were tied behind her back and her ankles were lashed together. For almost a full minute her incredulous position did not hit home. Then, panicking, she started sucking in air through her nose and felt the tickle of down. *There's a pillow case over my head!* She forced herself to calm down by slowly breathing. The distinct taste of blood mixed with the vague taste of detergent on a rough fabric identified a washcloth in her mouth Even though her tongue was swollen, she gently tried to nudge the cloth out of her mouth before she realized there was a strip of something caught in the corner of each side of her mouth and tied behind her head. Moving her tongue further split the sides of her mouth. Unless she had been out for hours, it had to be daylight. But wherever she was, it was pitch dark and she was moving. Not a car or train. Their movement was too distinctive. As if in answer to what, she suddenly felt the drop—an airplane! If they were going to get rid of her, they would have just killed her, not be transporting her somewhere. But who and where? Tony! Did he still have some idea she knew something?

Tears of frustration started to pour down. Realizing her nose was starting to become obstructed, she tried to stop. She sucked in air and blew it out, moving her head back and forth across the pillowslip. After doing this several times, she was able to breathe again, then she passed out.

When Susan awakened again someone was lifting her like a sack of potatoes and carrying her across what she thought was a tarmac. She must have been in the hold of the plane, but now the pillow case allowed her to see a glimpse of what might be runway lights in the distance. There were faint sounds of voices as she was tossed into the back of a car. But where? The night air had filled her lungs as she greedily sucked it in before the door was slammed. The sea. The cry of a sea gull confirmed her belief. Several people got into the car but no one near her. Wondering at this she finally figured they were in a limo. All of her questions were then simultaneously answered. Tony and the mob had brought her back to West Palm Beach.

Susan had unconsciously avoided thinking about her mother for years, but suddenly she wondered how her mother felt when she was told she had incurable cancer and would soon die. *But surely they chose a way of softening the news!* Susan felt as though she was caught up in some surreal experience that was connected to what she had experienced as a girl. The here and now grief that her mother surely must have felt now assailed her. Looking back, she realized how very self centered she was at that time—thinking only of herself and not understanding the pain and sorrow of anticipating one's own death. *Mother, I am so very sorry!*

Her emotional turmoil served to intensify the physical injury done to her as spasms of pain coursed through her. Her wrists, ankles, neck, and head throbbed. Knowing she would never see Jay again. Never have those five grandchildren that Julia wanted so badly. Never do all those things she had thought about in the last few weeks. Never feel Jay's arms around her and his lips on hers.

She thought: *The futility of the whole affair.* They would find out that she knew nothing, absolutely nothing about the mobs activities, but they would still have to kill her. So why—she suddenly stopped her thought mid-sentence. The word *affair* resonated in her mind—the affair she had catered. Of course! That was the only connection. Probably every member of the *organization* on the entire east coast was at that affair. Guilt by association? No! It had to be something she was witness to that even the FBI in Atlanta didn't know the right questions to ask about. But why would Tony risk going to so much trouble to bring her back to West Palm Beach? Why not just kill her? But isn't that what the man was supposed to have done? The limo stopped and Susan was unceremoniously half carried and half dragged inside a building.

A bright light was turned on as she was shoved into a chair. Forgetting she was stuffed and gagged and with the pillow case still in place, a man bent over in her face and asked in a voice hoarse and edgy, "Where's the necklace?" The man smelled of a mixture of musky sweat mingled with tobacco smoke and a hint of garlic. She felt light headed as she made a low croaking sound. Realizing she was gagged, he pulled the pillow case from her head and removed the gag. The man was medium height with skin like tanned leather. His hair was dark and coarse and streaked with gray. He had a prominent nose, and dark eyes that looked out from shaggy eyebrows that followed a low forehead. "Now answer me," he demanded with a snarl. She couldn't imagine what necklace he was talking about and sat looking at him dumbfounded. He backhanded her across the mouth causing an immediate gush of blood from her already swollen lips. As he brought back his hand to hit her again, she said, "Stop!" with such boldness, he did just that. The Irish ancestry would not allow her to go down without a fight. "I don't know who you are or even care. If you are doing this for Tony, he knows I don't have and never have had a necklace of his!" Susan knew she was about to die but was still surprised she had the ability and stamina to speak with such passion. The man walked away a few steps before walking back and hitting her again. Her head snapped back and she felt herself blacking out.

When she came to again, she knew someone had thrown water in her face as it dripped off her head and down her front. She wondered if she dared to involve anyone else. Surely someone had notified the police. Could she stall for time? Apparently there was a necklace that was critical to them. What about Tony? She made up her mind, blurting out, "I want to see Tony!"

~ 26 ~

The man looked at her and answered, "You wanna see him? You're gonna have to go straight to hell! Comprendre?" It took Susan a moment to understand. *Tony was dead!* The literal understanding did not really compute with her understanding of the words. Her visceral understanding was next as she felt a tight knot form in her stomach. Then the *real* meaning hit home. Her untenable position had dropped to impossible. Negotiate, negotiate her mind cried! But what with? What was this necklace? *Her voice was speaking, but it seemed to be removed from her,* "What are you planning to do with me once you have the necklace?" The man had not expected to deal with her, he expected to *deal* with her. He wanted to hit her again but was afraid the next blow might silence her forever, and he wouldn't get what he wanted This time when he turned and walked away he wanted her to experience the doubt. Was he prepared to hit her again? When he turned he realized she was not afraid. It took all of his will power not to hit her. If he did, he knew he was feeling such rage that this insignificant woman should defy him, that he would, without a question, kill her with his bare hands. But he was not the boss. There were others waiting for his call telling them he had the information.

"Okay," he said in his good cop voice. (hadn't he learned his lesson well?)

"Let's start over again Where is the necklace?" Susan knew intuitively that the information he was seeking was critical to the cartel. And, how she answered was critical to whether she lived another hour or not. She answered as someone would who was finally giving up information that they had held on to at the risk of death, "The necklace is in a safety deposit box in Martinsville." She had no idea where this would carry her. She just knew that he couldn't open a safety deposit box without her and held her breath as she awaited his reaction.

He walked a distance away and used a cell phone. When he came back he told one of the two men with him to stay. Then he left and was gone for a long time. On returning he said nothing to her as he cut the bindings off her hands and ankles. Then he finally spoke, "If you want to ever see your loverboy alive again you will do exactly as you are told. You say anything I don't tell you to say, he's dead. Do you understand?" Susan nodded her head in agreement even though her mind couldn't grasp what he had just told her. *They had Jay? No. No. No!* She realized he was instructing her what to say as he handed her the cell phone, " . . . . and tell her the two of you took off for a quick get-away and not to worry. You'll be back tomorrow." The phone was thrust in her hand.

"Wait! Wait! Tell me again what to say."

"Just do it!" There was a new edge to the menace in his voice.

No matter what he did to her, she had to ask, "Do you have Jay?"

"They told me you were smart. Do I have to draw you a picture?"

"Please. Tell me!" She persisted.

He wanted to hit her again but he couldn't afford to. They were already trying to find someone to clean her up for the trip to the bank. It was going to be daylight in a little while and the old lady might've already called the cops The flight from Savannah to the little airport outside of Atlanta wouldn't take long, but the ride into Martinsville would take over an hour. "Your man is alive. You wanna keep him that way? Call!"

It then occurred to Susan he meant her to call Julia. She heard Julia's worried voice answer on the third ring, "Hello."

"Hi Mrs. Martin," she said, "Jay's passed out from drinking too much, but I thought I'd better call so you wouldn't worry. We decided to take a quick trip and then just couldn't make it back home last night. Can you call his office and tell his secretary to cancel his appointments tomorrow . . . uh, today?. We'll be back in the early afternoon."

The silence that followed was frightening. The man jerked the phone away from Susan just as Julia grabbed her wits about her and answered, "Of course, dear. I'll call. Bye."

Susan had never been so grateful for her future mother-in-law's ability to see through obscure verbiage and ferret out what was relevant. The man, feeling satisfied the missing couple's disappearance was explained, led Susan stumbling back out to the limo. Walking was difficult due to the lack of circulation in her legs as he yanked her along. Even though it was still dark, Susan knew they weren't in West Palm Beach and yet somewhere near the sea. The scenery on the ride back to the airport confirmed that idea.

The plane was awaiting the passengers as they pulled up to a hangar on the outskirts of the main terminal. An oriental woman walked out of the building under the light as Susan was pulled into the plane. When she got on the plane where Susan had just been seated, she came over and opened a case equipped with medicine and makeup. Without comment she doctored Susan's lips and face until they were presentable. The woman spoke only the least number of words to insure Susan's compliance, then left without ever having made eye contact. *Hear no evil, see no evil, say no* evil.

The plane left in the dark, but before it banked west after takeoff, Susan could see the first faint glimmer of the sun on the horizon. The places on her face were numb where the woman had applied some ointment. Her lips felt as if they would crack open if she smiled—not that she had any reason to smile. She again thought of her mother and wondered which would be the more difficult position—to know you were dying and try to keep your morale up for your family's sake, or do what she was doing now—prolonging her own life at the possible risk of her family. *But they had already kidnapped Jay!* Then realizing she was beating herself up mentally, she *censured her over-developed conscience!*

They landed at another small airport north of Atlanta. Having been allowed to sit in a passenger seat on the return trip, she recognized the skyline. The return trip had been almost nice after her previous treatment. But she could now identify everyone . . . another indication she was marked for demise, and Jay would be disposed of also. *She was totally helpless.* There was a sense of pathos flirting with her mind as it seeped into all the nooks and crannies that housed all her plans of work and love and children. She felt a tear drop on her plastered cheek and then it hit her—anger. Her heart started pumping as the adrenaline was released into her blood stream and a thought kept going through her mind as they herded her into the car at the airport. *I will not allow them to get away with this . . . I will not allow them to get away with this.* These words became her mantra as they left the airport. The sign at the front read MCCUL, then a large tree blocked the rest of the name. A blindfold was placed on her after they rode down a parkway. The switch to what seemed like an expressway by an acceleration lane was followed by a series of turns and loops to the sound of a gravel road. When they finally stopped, she was pulled out of the limo and led into a house that had a musty odor. Once inside, her blindfold was removed and she recognized the interior of a spacious log cabin.

Jay, sat tied to a chair. There was a bruise around one eye and a cut and abrasions that showed through the five o'clock shadow of stubble on his face. The man seated across from the table from him had an automatic pistol lying in front of the him. When Jay looked at Susan, she saw the intake of breath as he realized the extent of her injuries. *Don't, Jay, Don't! Her* eyes tried to communicate. His jaw became set and he seemed to settle back down in the chair. Before she was pulled away his eyebrow went up and he winked.

While the men completed their plans in another room, Susan was forced into a chair facing away from Jay. She wondered if Julia had called the police. Within ten minutes she was herded back outside, this time to Jay's car. A man got into the seat beside her, someone she had not seen previously. His taffy colored hair emphasized his ruddy completion. That, coupled with a wide mouth that spread across his abundant supply of teeth gave him the look of a jack-o-lantern. His voice sounded like your local generic weatherman when he spoke, "Ms. Sullivan, you will do exactly as I say or you won't ever see Mr. Martin again. Do you understand his life is literally in your hands?" Susan had not spoken a word since the woman had made up her face in . . . . Savannah?

She now spoke, trying not to move her swollen lips, "Yeth."

If he noticed the lisp, he ignored it and went on with his directions. "Before we get to the outskirts of Martinsville, I am transferring to the car behind us. So listen very carefully. Where is the key to your safety deposit box?" Susan answered slowly, as if reluctant to pass on the information, "It's . . . . it's in my dresser in my bedroom"

"You will go in and get the key. If Mrs. Martin is there, placate her, then leave." He continued, "You will then take the key to the bank and remove the locket from your safety deposit box and bring it to me. I will be waiting in the same spot where I will leave you. Is that clear?" Susan's head was throbbing. Her mind was like a fly caught suddenly in a spider web. The word *locket* was the web. *The necklace they have been talking about is my locket.* Then she remembered. *The party she catered for the Vascolas!* The man's impatient voice broke through. "Ms. Sullivan. Do you understand?"

"Yes, absolutely," she said to him—but silently—*I understand so much more than you do!*

Susan had made the trip blindfolded, so could not see as they stopped at an old church outside of town and drove around in the back to a small cemetery. There were huge oaks that hid both cars from the road. As they stopped, the man removed the blindfold. For the first time in twenty-four hours she felt hope. She didn't quite understand it all yet, but at least she knew what they wanted. Then she looked at the gravestones and shivered. *Had they too had hope in the face of death?*

~ 27 ~

No sooner had Julia gotten off the line with Susan, then the magnitude of the problem hit her. She found Bruce Nesmith's home phone number his mother had given her and was about to call when it occurred to her if someone could abduct Susan and Jay in broad daylight in a small town like Martinsville, they were capable of anything. She took her cell phone out of her purse and called Bruce. A sleepy but slightly gruff voice answered, "Yeah." Then spotting Martinsville on the caller ID, he changed his voice to an alert concerned tone, "Julia? Jay? What is going on?"

"Bruce, someone has kidnapped Jay and Susan."

Julia heard his intake of breath before he asked, "Are you on your cell phone?"

"Yes."

"Are they asking for ransom?"

"No. Susan called me in the wee hours this morning. She called me Mrs. Martin and said she and Jay had driven out of town but Jay was too drunk to drive back so they decided to spend the night. She asked that I have his secretary cancel his appointments for today, then ended the call abruptly. I looked for the number afterward, but it was blocked."

Bruce Nesmith's training overcame his personal tie. "Julia, start from the beginning and tell me what led up to this."

"Susan had an attempt on her life two nights ago. We . . . uh, the man was caught and jailed. Susan was okay and insisted on going through with a catering commitment on Saturday. On Sunday morning Jay and I left Susan in bed to rest and went to church. I went to the hospital directly after church and didn't get home until late afternoon and thought Jay and Susan were off somewhere relaxing. I went to bed early and received the call about four thirty this morning."

Bruce Nesmith knew Jay Martin was not one to overdo his alcohol. Julia was right. Something was going on. "Have you called in the local law?" He thought carefully how he worded his next request knowing how loyal Julia was to her people in Martinsville. "Julia, please don't call anyone until I get there. I need to speak to the locals before they do *anything.* Will you promise me this?" Julia's answer came over the line like a sigh, "Of course." He assured her he would be in Martinsville in less than two hours by car; a helicopter would draw too much attention, then got her cell phone number before he hung up. Julia sat on the side of the bed and wondered if it were possible for someone to have bugged the phone. Everything she knew about such things could be summed up in one sentence—a short one at that. Then the terrible awareness that Jay's and Susan's lives were in her hands brought to mind her deceased husband and those first weeks after his death so many years ago. This was the first time she felt the horrible loss of his counsel since that time. *I am not as strong as even I think I am!*

Julia's forte was her ability to move forward. When something needed to be done—she didn't question whether or not she could do—she just did it! She stood up and walked to her bathroom, took her shower, dressed, went to the kitchen as usual and made breakfast. She then read the paper while having a second cup of coffee. If anyone had asked her what she had read, she would have been uncertain. Finally at eight forty-five she called Jay's office and told his secretary to cancel his appointments for the day. Afterward she went to the library where she made plans for her possible absence and waited to hear from Bruce. She started to pull a book on kidnapping but thought better of it. *I am at the edge now. I must not go over it!*

Two hours later Julia was startled to look up into the face of Bruce Nesmith. He placed his finger over his mouth, then pleasantly asked her, "Are you Mrs. Martin by any chance? She drew in a deep breath before she answered, "Yes. May I help you?" Bruce gave an approving wink and continued the charade. "Yes, Bill Britain here. I understand you are looking to update your computer system and would like to show what my company has to offer. We specialize in library software."

Julia stood up extending her hand and clasped Bruce's anxiously. "I'm so glad to meet you Mr. Britain. Please, let's go into my office where we want disturb anyone." Bruce followed Julia into her office where he sat down opposite her desk. He took out some papers from his briefcase, saying, "I hope I don't overwhelm you with too much information at one time. Not to suggest you aren't capable of understanding. It's just that the industry is glutted with new technology." As he was saying this the piece of paper he placed before her read: "We know this is bigger than even we imagined. We may be dealing with bugs. I have gone by the police station and talked to them. Hang on and *please follow our directives!* There's a good chance of getting Jay and Susan back alive if we remain calm."

Julia was best when given a challenge. She had never had a greater challenge than now. The word *bugs* had stumped her for a second "This looks very suitable for our purposes Mr. Britain. Can you show me exactly how these separate systems will interface?" Bruce thought of Julia as a privileged woman whose education and breeding had prepared her for roles that required prestige and social grace, but certainly *not* for cool savvy. He found himself tongue-tied from the shear strain of dealing with someone so intimately connected to himself. Someone he now realized he did not really know! The truth that his mother had staunchly reiterated for twenty years *ad nauseam* now hit home: Julia Martin was fine as gold, tough as steel, and as brilliant as a diamond.

Fortified with his new opinion of Julia, he answered, "I see no problem in demonstrating that; however, I would like to run through the basic program and then show how all the different facets merge later." The next note he handed her read, "Have you heard from the perps?" He gave her a moment before he asked, "Will you be needing the program anytime soon?" "No," Julia replied. The next item was critical. "Have you any idea where in the vicinity they could keep S. and J. without someone spotting them?" Bruce waited a minute to give anyone monitoring them the impression that Julia was reading a document, but Julia spoke up, "Mr. Britain, I think you have the potential for solving our problems. We haven't explored other systems before so I haven't the vaguest idea how your system compares with others, both technologically and cost-wise. It's true we are a small town and may not seem to require all the items in a program found in a large city library, but this is a large county that we serve and *there are miles and miles of roads where farms are tucked away."*

Bruce didn't know quite what he had expected Julia to reply to his last question, but the present means of communication were hopeless. There were lines that normally didn't show around her eyes and mouth and the pen she held so tightly in her hand caused her knuckles to blanche white. He looked at his watch. "It's not quite eleven. Would you do me the honor of having an early lunch with me?" There seemed to be a knot that had been miraculously untied in Julia's body. The tension lifted, leaving her face with a calm and peaceful look. The resolve was still there, but the strain gone as she answered, "I would be delighted. And if you don't mind my suggesting it, I know just the place to satisfy the most particular palate. Give me just a moment to let my staff know."

Bruce escorted Julia to her car; the decision for her to drive having been mutually agreed upon. She thought about the 007 movies she had watched with Jay in his teenage years. The world of fantasy had now spilled over into the real world. Bugs were no longer just insects but now included small electronic devices. As they reached her car, Julia thought of her long-time friend from college, Bruce's mother. *Poor Dotty. How had she managed to keep her mind all these years with Bruce running around pursuing criminals?*

The thought of eating was not possible with Susan and Jay in danger, but the fact that whoever these men were that had her children couldn't bug the whole town filled her with a certainty that they would be defeated. By the time Julia and Bruce pulled into the parking lot of Maison du Apperitif, they knew they had two roles to play; one they were already playing, and the other, as strategists, would be just as critical What they needed was a plan.

The small building wedged in the line of other buildings on the main street was as unique in design as the couple who ran the restaurant it housed. The façade was what might be referred to as Americanized Rococo. Built in the late nineteenth century when materials and labor were cheap, it had stood the test of time. Less ornate than its cousin of the preceding century in Europe, its less pretentious bearing made it a jewel to even the unschooled. The couple who ran the restaurant were refugees from Viet Nam and trained in French cooking. Both Bruce and Julia ordered the 'Soupe du Jour' and carefully exchanged information. Julia knew the people of the area, Bruce knew about dealing with the criminal mind. When they left the restaurant, a plan was finished but not their soup.

~ 28 ~

Tom Jeter knew the county better than the police, the Postal Service, the farmers, real estate folks, better than anyone. As a boy he had bought every book he could find on birds, on local wild life, then finally on historical sites—particularly Civil War sites. The best years of his life had been spent teaching these things to Boy Scouts. After he married he gave up scouting due to complaints from his wife. Several years later when she ran off and left him for another man, he felt too embarrassed to go back to scouting—instead he started cataloging the birds, wild-life, and Civil War sites of the area. No one realized, but he had been published in several magazines. He kept himself up financially by doing odd jobs for the senior citizens in the area. He knew people thought him an oddity, but it didn't matter. Most were kind.

Today Tom had no jobs to do, so had headed out to the northern part of the county to try to locate a bivouac that was mentioned in an obscure account he had run across in a Civil War diary. By chance he had come across the disreputable looking journal while cleaning out a root cellar in a formidable old house built in the late mid-nineteenth century and now occupied by the last of kin—an elderly woman. Numerous generations of the family had lived and contributed their clutter to the nightmarish assemblage of junk. The old woman told Tom she would pay him a small sum of money to clear our the cellar and do whatever he wanted with the contents. Tom was sure everything would be hauled to the dump but felt sorry for the old woman and took on the job. When he found the diary, he offered it to her, but she refused, saying, “It’s yours.”

Tom took the diary home and spent several days figuring out the unschooled writing before he realized it was a relic from the Civil War. A description of an encampment was all it took to decide him to pour over county maps for the exact location.

After spending days in the county survey office, Tom finally figured out about where the site was located. Early Monday morning he was tramping through the woods when he found the site, no difficult task for a trained individual. Teaching the scouts orienteering had been an especially gratifying accomplishment for him and his expertise later served in his hobbies. Grown men were known to die within a short distance of help because they lacked this skill, though it was second nature to a man who loved being out in the woods. Thus it was a shock when he heard the sound of car tires slipping on loose gravel in what he had assumed was a remote area. He walked in the direction of the sound and found himself looking down a slope at a cabin. There was a limo (unusual for this locale) and a car that he recognized because of the license tag-USAF 1990. Jay Martin’s car.

Tom watched as a woman he recognized as Susan was led from the limo with a blindfold on. Tom wasn’t a dumb man—just a simple man who had isolated himself from the world with hobbies, and as he stood watching, he tried to make sense of what was happening below, when suddenly, not even sure why, he ducked behind a bush and continued to watch.

What was going on? Tom knew intuitively this was something sinister. The men had pistols. Criminals? Whatever was happening below, he was determined to see more. Tom removed his boots, leaving on his socks and worked his way down the slope behind the cabin. He took each step carefully to avoid making a sound. There was a window too high to peer through. He found a wooden bucket and turned it upside down and carefully eased himself up until he could peer inside the cabin. Four men were in the room. Jay Martin was tied to a chair and looked roughed up. Susan was pushed into a chair that was turned towards the wall. One man, with a pistol lying in front of him, sat at a table across from Jay. Three of the men started to have a pow wow over in a far corner, then looking over at Jay, left the room. Tom continued to watch, even though he knew it was dangerous.

When the men came back out into the main room, it was evident the conference was over, so Tom slipped down off the bucket and quickly hid under some bushes next to the front side of the house. A tall man with sandy colored came out with Susan, pushing her into the front seat of Jay's car, then got into the driver's seat. Another man came out and got behind the wheel of the limo following Jay's car as it was driven off.

Tom realized he had a choice—go get help and take a chance on what might happen while he was gone or, somehow, help get Jay out of there. But they had guns. He hated guns! The scales had tipped just little. One against two instead of four. As he planned his next move he only hoped Jay remembered the bird calls taught two decades ago. The sound of the Wood Thrush warbled from his throat. Tom gave it a little more volume than usual to catch Jay's attention. He moved back around to the window and called again, this time giving it a more plaintive sound just in case Jay didn't recognize the call. Satisfied that Jay had heard, he pushed the bucket in place and stepped up to look. Jay was turned at a thirty degree angle to the window, and as he turned his head, he saw Tom. The one man was still sitting in front of Jay and his body was at a right angle to the window. The other man was not in sight. Jay's look was foreboding and Tom sensed, rather than heard, the man as he came up on his rear. Easing himself off the bucket, he imagined he felt the man's breath on his neck as his arm shot up while he twisted, ducking his head. The butt of the gun caught his arm. Surprised, the man lost his balance as Tom hit him in the gut causing the gun to go off. Then Tom, fighting to wrest the gun from the man's grasp, tripped on the bucket and careened into the man. The gun went off again into the man's chest as Tom grabbed with both hands.

By this time Jay's guard came running out of the cabin waving a gun as his partner fell at Tom's feet. The first shot the second gunman got off went wild, but the next one caught Tom in the gut. Jay, having managed to stand and break the chair he was tied to, came running out just as Tom was hit. He tackled the gunman from the rear. Both men sprawled on the ground. Tom staggered over and stood while Jay struggled with the second man. Afraid he might hit Jay, Tom aimed at the man's leg, fired the gun then continued to stand, wobbling but refusing to fall. Tom's aim found its mark as the blast of the bullet tore the man's leg apart. His scream echoed through the woods. Then he went limp. Jay got up and checked the other man. Dead! Next he checked Tom, who, unaware of the severity of his wound, stood ready to continue the fight, oblivious of the blood oozing down the front of his trousers.

Jay had to speak to him several times to get him into a prone position where he removed his own shirt, folded it and pushed it up under Tom's shirt to try to slow the bleeding. By this time, Jay knew unless Tom received medical attention immediately, he'd bleed to death.

Jay leaned down with his face almost touching Tom's and spoke in a loud voice to the now comatose man, "Tom, wake up. I need to know where your truck is." After no response from Tom, Jay found Tom's keys walked up the slope above the cabin and looked around. A spot of red showed through the trees. *Was it his imagination—wishful thinking?* Whatever he thought could only be proved by closer observation. If it was the truck, it was on another hill about a half mile away. Heavy going. He took a deep breath then started a dead run in that direction. He fell once, tripping over vines, then a branch caught him across the temple biting into a cut., but the pain was nothing compared to the exhilaration of coming to a clearing and seeing the truck. When he got in, he realized it was miles back to the road that would lead to the cabin. *He had to take the chance of driving through the woods the way he came!* He started off slowly, speeding up as the terrain allowed. The going was rough and Jay was afraid at any moment he would bust a tire.

When he got to the slope above the cabin he stopped and debated before driving to the edge, then he let it go. As the truck careened down, fearful that applying the brakes would flip the it over, he hit them just before he crashed into the shrubbery next to the house. His head hit the sun visor cushioning the blow as he was thrown into the windshield. Still stunned, he stumbled over where Tom lay and hoisted him onto his back, then carried him to the back of the camper where he pulled him into the back and wrapped him in a blanket. Disoriented by the blow to his head, he sat a moment to figure out which direction to go. Several times over the years he had seen the log cabin. Then it hit him. *The old Muller place!* The wheels spun as hit the accelerator. Finally, he was back on the road where he had been so many times in his life and headed for the hospital.

Five miles down the road he was intercepted by a deputy sheriff who recognized him and led him to the hospital. The people in the emergency room were waiting to take Tom to the OR. As the gurney was whisked away, Jay thought about Susan. He quickly went back to the patrol car where the young officer was talking on his radio. Jay knew he would be placing Susan's life in jeopardy if he revealed what was happening. He had to talk to Mac first. He leaned over and spoke to the officer who had escorted him in, Jim Little from the county. "I need to raise Mac in town on your radio. May I?" The young officer was caught between correct police procedure and gut intuition. "Yes, sir," He replied before turning and saying, "Get in the passenger seat." Jay had always had great respect for Mac *but to entrust him with Susan's life?*

When Jay got off the radio with Mac he felt for the first time in twenty-four hours that there was a good chance of getting through this madness that had been wrought—by who? No. Not who but hooligans as his grandfather would say. To give them a name would be assigning them the dignity of human beings. They were like cockroaches that did their mischief under the cover of darkness or clandestine means. Jay suddenly realized how angry he was! When they hit him, threatened his life, and finally told of abducting Susan, he had kept reminding himself that he was not going to allow them to destroy his judgment and shake his sense that justice would prevail.

Having vented a little, Jay was amused at his naiveté. True that he certainly hadn't tried any murder cases in the last five years, but he was acquainted enough with that seedy group of characters whose lack of integrity made it possible for the crime syndicate to operate and prosper. And he was loath to admit that he personally, from time to time, found himself having to rub shoulders with a few of them. That's why, when he heard Susan's story of her affair with Tony Vascola, he believed her to be innocent. *Sometimes it is hard to distinguish between mushrooms and toadstools until you are poisoned or dying.* The thought of the word *dying* jolted Jay. Mac told him that Bruce and his men had taken over, and Susan would be protected. The last thing he had warned Jay about was the possibility of being seen. That would certainly blow the FBI's cover and endanger Susan. But to sit and wait, doing nothing was agony for Jay.

He went back into the hospital to await Mac's call and finally leaned back with his hands behind the back of his head. Frequently after a hard day in court he practiced the breathing practice taught in a Yoga class he'd taken years ago. He did this now. A peace permeated his whole body as he envisioned Susan in a flowing green dress walking through Julia's rose garden. His daydream was shattered by someone shaking him. "Mr. Martin. Mr. Martin?" a voice asked, "Can you hear me?" Jay opened his eyes and responded in a calm and sonorous voice that belied the sudden rush of adrenaline and testosterone that was coursing through his blood, "Yes."

"Dr. Jessup said to tell you that Tom's status is considered critical, but he is extremely optimistic. He said he didn't know of Tom having any kin but thought you would want to know." Jay recognized the young man talking to him but couldn't recall his name and, as was his habit, searched in his mind trying to bring the name to memory, then realized the poor soul was waiting to be dismissed. *Bingo!*

"Ted, I appreciate your taking the time to relay this good news from Dr. Jessup. Thank you very much and please give Dr. Jessup my best regards." Ted left with just a little more spring to his step than before.

~ 29 ~

When Susan looked around, there was a grave being dug on the backside of the old cemetery by two men with a truck parked nearby. Her blindfold was apparently removed just in time to avoid detection, and the workers assumed the limo and car were members of the decease's family overseeing the gravesite preparation. The man beside her had not spoken since his instructions back at the cabin. He cleared his throat before saying, "Ms. Sullivan, if you wish to see your lover again you will do exactly as I tell you. We will take you out to the cabin after we get what we want and you will be left there until we are well out of the country. We are not concerned that you've seen us, so you will be allowed to live *if you behave yourself.* Do you understand?"

Susan knew better, but answered, "Yes, I understand."

"Good. Now here is what you will do. Go to the Martin home and get the key to the safety deposit box; then go to the bank and retrieve the locket. We have timed the trip and know just how long this will take. You will be back out here in thirty minutes or your Mr. Martin will die. If you encounter anyone who wants to detain you, I think you're a creative enough woman to avoid this without suspicion. Do you have any questions?"

Susan's mind was frantically trying to take in what the man was saying and wondered if they had actually timed the trip. Surely it would take more time. The only thing that gave her hope was the fact that they *thought* the locket was in the safety deposit box. It was in her jewelry box under the little velvet flap. It had kept getting tangled on her other pieces, so she'd pushed it under the flap. But why hadn't they found it? She answered her own question. *They had abducted her in daylight and had been in a hurry!* The extra minutes she could avoid in the depository area might give her an edge. *But what if they had someone stationed in the bank to keep an eye on her*? She couldn't take a chance on Jay's life. At least she actually had a safety deposit box! And surely Julia had alerted the police. Before she could say anything, the man had slipped out of the car and retreated toward the limo, saying just within earshot, "See you in thirty minutes, dear."

Susan started the car and looked at the gravestones as she drove past, wondering. *Did they too have hope in the face of death?* Exiting the cemetery, she drove within the speed limit and observed the time as she pulled into the Martin driveway—eleven minutes. She was so nervous she bungled unlocking the door that slowly opened to reveal a pale-faced Julia, who hugged her and asked, "Susan dear, did Jay go to his office?" Before Susan could answer, Julia placed her finger across her mouth and shook her head. Susan quickly pushed back from Julia and started to her room, answering, "No, Jay went to see some client he missed this morning. I've got to hurry to the bank Julia. See you later." Susan quickly removed her locket from its hiding place, and the safety deposit key was in the bottom of the lingerie drawer where she had left it. *Thank God!*

The parking places were taken up in the front of the bank so she was forced to park on the far side. Her internal clock said *another minute lost!* Once inside, everyone seemed to be busy. Susan's throat was dry and her hands perspired. *What can I do?* A man exited a room and approached her that she remembered from . . . . where? The Russell building in Atlanta . . . . An FBI agent! "May I help you Ms. Sullivan?" He asked as though he had done business with her every day. "Yes, I need to get into my safety deposit box."

He quickly produced a slip for her to fill out then guided her into the safety deposit box room. She glanced at her watch. Only thirteen minutes left. There were too many people she didn't know. How could she be sure she wasn't being watched? Walking over to the safety deposit boxes, she felt the tears hitting her cheeks before the agent said under his breath, "Mr. Martin's fine." Susan looked up as if she had somehow managed to hear something she desperately wanted to hear but had misunderstood. "What—did you say?" she asked.

The agent looked at her and said, "You're doing great. Don't lose it now. There's someone out there in the bank and we don't know who, but they're part of this. Keep it together for a little longer." Susan turned and left the bank. As she started to pull away from the curb, someone was tapping at the passenger door. The woman looked vaguely familiar. Susan hit the window switch. *I can't ignore her. Another minute lost!* As the window rolled down the woman said, "Susan, you may not remember me, but we met at the reception recently. May I speak to you just a moment?" Susan wanted to scream no, but before she could answer, two FBI agents appeared on either side of her and took her arm. She brought her elbow back but the agents were too well trained and kept her subdued until she calmed down. Thinking she would offer no more resistance, they relaxed and started leading her away. Susan was too involved in her race against time to wonder at the agents rash treatment of an innocent person and tried to pull away. *I must get back to Jay!* The woman slammed her purse into the agent on the left, then turning, kneed the other in the groin. Before they were able to stop her, she tried to open Susan's door. Susan accelerated, throwing the woman to the pavement, then managed to pull out into the traffic. She didn't know whether to laugh or cry. A song her father used to sing ran through her memory: *I've got a tiger by the tail it's plain to see.* Then she started to cry, realizing she was making jokes when people's lives were at stake. She made no effort to stem the tears and when she was pulled over four blocks away, Mac was at her window, "You okay?" He asked. Before answering she asked, "Where is Jay?" Mac knew if he told her Jay was at the hospital she would jump to conclusions, so he replied, "He's gonna be just fine when he finds out you are."

"Then I'm not fine. I'm great. So please let me go see him." Mac was still caught. "Tell you what, Ms. Sullivan."—Susan interjected, "Please, it's Susan." "Okay, Susan, then I'm Mac. I'm taking you to the Martin home where Jay is meeting us. Ms. Julia's promised to have a dish of peach cobbler with vanilla ice cream on top. Deal?" Susan thought *how like Julia to offer food,* then said, "Absolutely. But I'll drive Jay's car. Okay?" Mac walked off, his voice trailing behind him, "Follow me." As soon as he got into his car, he called the hospital and spoke to Jay.

Driving home, Susan had the eerie feeling she was occupying someone else's body . . . . *No, that's not it. I feel like someone put me in a blender and then poured me out into a mold.* She wondered if it was fatigue that would go away after a few days or if she would ever be that in-control, totally rational person who calmly made decisions without *all this maudlin boo-hooing!* Somewhere, in the back of her highly rational and analytical mind, bits and pieces of Psy 101 formed a collage that penetrated her subconscious mind, and—even if it didn't arrive as a conclusion except subliminally—she let herself off the hook. The thought of seeing Jay once again occupied her mind—and there he sat on the front steps as she entered the driveway!. He stood up and started walking toward her as she got out of the car and started up the walkway.

"Are you alright?" His voice sounded slightly whispery. Reaching her, he gently took her by the shoulders as though fearful of breaking something and pulled her to his chest, burying his face in the cloud of red hair at her neck. For a moment he said nothing as he felt her hot tears streaming down her face. Then he said quietly, "I think we need to get busy on those five kids as soon as we can. Okay?" Susan didn't answer. But she didn't have to. The body really does have a language all its own.

~ 30 ~

The Monday following Jay and Susan's abduction and rescue was full of questions raised by the town's people of Martinsville. The previous Saturday night groups that attended various week-end functions—including the reception out at the country club Susan had catered for Mildred Brice—were unaware of what had occurred out on Ralph Getz's farm that day. Even as people dressed to go out that night, the two very different dramas were at different stages of development.

On the Saturday before the kidnapping, one of the calves turned up missing on the farm adjacent to the Getz farm. The owner, Roland Jarrett, went out looking for the calf; finally, after no luck, he wandered over into Ralph's pasture. Roland had lost a number of cattle over the years to what he referred to as *the black hole* on Ralph's farm. He told close friends, "Ralph oughta have a slogan—*Getz gets um!*"

While out near the well where Pinky was dumped, Roland thought about the possibility that his calf had fallen into the well so went over and looked down into the well. The top had long-ago disappeared. Heavy timbers had been placed around the opening, some rotting. The smell convinced Roland that *something* was down in the well but not his calf. It takes an animal at least two days to start to rot. He decided to call the sheriff. Roland knew Ralph was in the hospital and would probably go to jail when released, but this was Randy's call and he was sometimes a little territorial concerning a division of jurisdiction between city and county law enforcement.

As it turned out, Randy Collier was more than delighted to come out to Ralph Getz's farm. Especially now that Ralph was under the gun of Mac. Randy arrived within a half hour followed by an entourage of deputies and the local wrecker service. One of the younger, more ambitious deputies volunteered to go down in the well after the more seasoned officers got a whiff of the odor.

When the corpse of Pinky was laid out on the ground, no one recognized him. The well had some water from rain, but was basically dry. The lime dumped in by Ralph had served to do a sort of blotchy fixation of the features of his face by keeping the flies from laying their larva. Pinky would be transported to the morgue until identification was verified by the items inside in a travel bag found after the body was removed from the well. Unfortunately, the young deputy was again called upon to make the second descent after someone spotted the bag. The sheriff remembered the contraband found in Ralph Getz's truck the night he was attacked and was willing to bet his next paycheck the victim figured in some way with that. He decided to go into town and see if he couldn't get the corpse's fingerprints and check the data base for an ID. Mac would probably be at that big shindig tonight and he'd be doing him a favor. It chafed Randy that Mac was invited to affairs that shunned him—especially since he'd had four years of college. Mac's dad had been the police chief twenty years before Mac's appointment to that position. The ole buddy system trumped education every time!

When Randy and his group had pulled back onto the highway headed into town, Roland Jarrett had again assumed his search for his calf. *A strange person. He just found a murdered man and now he walks away.* Randy refused to turn on his siren. The boys would be disappointed but he wanted to keep everything low-key until he'd finished *his* investigation. Sure enough, as he had predicted, Mac had left the station early—seems he had a big engagement to attend tonight. After getting the corpse's fingerprints, Randy left for his office. An hour and a half elapsed before he finally gave up his search for a match on the fingerprints. There were two driver's licenses found in the corpse's belongings. One turned out to be bogus and the other had not so much as a parking violation. But at least the man was identified. Next he tried the cell phone. He realized how out of touch he was with all he'd learned in school. The damn battery was dead and he had to locate a cord that would fit so he could recharge it. He left his office and headed for the local Radio Shack. The shop owner had already closed and was figuring up his day's receipts when he knocked on his door and told him what he wanted. Fifteen minutes later he was back in his office and had the phone hooked up charging. Two hours? Time to go home to supper.

The news about the man found in the well had started to travel through the town. By the time Jay and Susan were safe on Monday afternoon, the news was in the Martinsville Chronicle. Some people tied the two separate incidences together, sure that somehow Susan was involved. Rumors ran rampant, and Julia, realizing that even the Martin name could not stem the speculation that had started like a virus and mushroomed into almost a pandemic, knew she had to make a statement that would satisfy both the curious and those smaller, more malignant minds. William Shakespeare had decided four hundred years before that whether it concerned telling the truth or fighting, one must always use discretion. Willie had been one of her guiding sources of wisdom for all of her adult life. Too much information gave too many opportunities for wrong inferences and secrecy also posed deadly consequences to reputations. The Martinsville Chronicle had already gone to press on Monday about the body found in Ralph's well. Rumor and speculation needed to be quelled.

Julia, Jay, and Susan had a meeting on Tuesday with Dave Biggs, owner and editor of the Chronicle. Dave was given an abridged version of Susan's and Jay's kidnapping and asked to keep it contained as much as his journalistic bent would allow him due to the kidnappers being involved with a large crime syndicate under investigation. Julia knew the FBI had not disclosed the nature of the information on the micro chip found behind the picture in Susan's locket and at the present time an on-going investigation would be jeopardized if the cartel knew the FBI had possession of the chip. Dave Biggs was told nothing of the existence of the micro chip nor of Susan's direct involvement with Tony Vascola. Anything he wrote as a result of this meeting would put him in the position of printing an explanation that would satisfy people but certainly wouldn't be a cover-up. *One can not tell what one does not know!* The most exciting thing he had ever written was an *expose'* of political corruption in the next county twenty years before.

Julia found it easier to trust Dave to print what they had given him than to allow speculation to continue. He agreed to write the story as a kidnapping case and simply not mention the crime cartel. The prisoners were taken back to Atlanta for further questioning and the two dead men were transported to the morgue at the Federal Prison, relieving the town of outside nosey reporters. Tom was expected to recover and later would bask in the glow of his heroism embellished by Dave's writing of the shoot-out. Fortunately, the national wire services had been kept at bay. Julia and Jay were anticipating future murmurings but felt time would soon dissapate these. And, after the next series of events, time lost out to sensationalism.

After Ralph had recovered from his concussion, he tried to see Vera and was refused admittance to her room. He was then charged with battery and taken to jail by Mac who later also charged him with murder when it had been determined the blood on the floor of his building matched the blood of the corpse found in his well. On Monday Vera was transported to a hospital in Atlanta where she was to undergo plastic surgery on her nose and face. Julia had called Dotty Nesmith and asked her to make sure Vera had good doctors, including a psychiatrist.

On Tuesday night, as Julia, Jay, and Susan were having a glass of wine in the sunroom, no one seemed to have much to say; not to mean that there was any strain or hint of tension. Far from it. There was an atmosphere born of understanding that is usually found in old companions of many years. Jay got up. "Another glass anyone?" Julia and Susan both spoke almost simultaneously, the two voices echoing, "Yes please." "Yes please." After the second glass was finished, Susan remarked, "During all the excitement of the past week, I've forgotten to ask what is going on with Henry and Velma?" Julia cleared her throat . . . Susan held her breath and waited for the answer. Good? Bad? Julia, obviously moved emotionally, answered, "I'm pleased to say that they have Henry on a new drug and they say he is more lucid and calm than they have seen him in the last couple of years. Velma has finally gotten some rest and is more like her old self again. Five years ago she would be sick to have missed all the excitement of our little town of the last few days; however, I've seen fit not to tell her until later. Now, what do you kids think about planning a wedding for a month from now? I think I need to push for my grandchild before anything else happens!" Jay and Susan were not about to argue with the future grandmother of their children!